PUNK RULES OK

PUNK RULES OK

CHRIS WALTER

BURN BOOKS LTD.

10 9 8 7 6 5 4 3 2 1

Published by Burn Books Ltd.
Vancouver, British Columbia

Printed and bound in Canada

**National Library of Canada Cataloguing in Publication
Data**

Walter, Chris, 1959-
  Punk rules ok

  ISBN 0-9730293-0-7

  I. Title.
PS8595.A595P86 2002 C813'.6 C2002-910007-0
PR9199.4.W34P86 2002

*Someday punk is gonna be
really big and we'll all be famous.*
Dimwit, Subhumans, '82

01

Paula slid open the patio doors and stepped onto the balcony. A salty warm tang blew in from the harbour. Winter was dead. A sudden awareness of life made her skin tingle as she absorbed the moist Pacific air. With inner fires burning, she gazed at the distant snow capped mountains and dreamed secret dreams.

"Oi!" bellowed a drunk voice from the living room. "Bring me a beer!"

Tranquillity was shattered. The baron of beer was thirsty. Again. The contrast between the beauty of the mountains and the obnoxiousness of her house guest was a shock. "Get yer own beer, you lazy shit. Is *Elvis* tied to your ass?" It was not Paula's nature to suffer quietly.

What Meatboy really wanted was some pussy, but for now he would settle with beer. The empty can in his hands was deader than Jerry Garcia. Now if Paula would just haul her sexy butt off the balcony and get him another, life would be sweet. "C'mon baby, I love you." It was easier to talk than walk.

Paula wasn't buying Meatboy's bullshit. All he loved was drinking and fucking; no particular brand of beer, and no particular girl. His allegiances were simple—he had none. "Listen shithead," she said sharply. "I'll get you another beer when you prove clams have legs." She was going to have to find a way to cut this visit short.

"Gawdamn!" complained Meatboy. "Clams don't have legs!" He felt since he had bought the beer, Paula should fetch it for him. After all, fair was fair. He fired his empty beer can at her, which whistled past her head and began its gravity bound descent to the courtyard twelve floors below.

Paula studied the missile thrower from her perch on the balcony and wondered what had attracted her to this drunken sloth in the first place. It sure wasn't his personal hygiene. She wished she'd never screwed Meatboy. Now that she'd seen his dick, she didn't want to see it again. The smell of the warming earth pulled her attention back to the snowy mountains, her eyes misting over.

Meatboy sulked. If there was one thing he couldn't stand it was being ignored. The last time he was in town Paula had been more than friendly — now she didn't even seem interested in him. It looked like he was going to have to get his own beer, forget getting laid.

At twenty-seven Meatboy felt he had reached the summit of punk-rawkness. Grossly exaggerated tales of his wild exploits were bandied about from coast to coast by a new generation of young punks—most of them still naive enough to think punk was about getting dressed up nice and pointy on Friday night. His experience and reputation were becoming increasingly hard to live up to, but he figured he could still sniff glue or slam dance better than any of those little Blink-182 faggots. How could Paula resist his obvious charms? The draft from the open patio door carried her scent to him and he admitted to himself that he really dug that raggedy-ass little bitch. Giving Paula a hungry look, he got reluctantly to his feet. She was cuter than a six-pack all covered with dew.

Paula revelled in her power over the Big Bad Punk Rocker. Hoisting herself up on the railing, she spread her legs in an inviting, tight leather smile. As Meatboy stepped forward to claim his prize, she snapped the trap shut and left him standing there like a slavering idiot. Confused, he tried to figure out what he had done. "What the hell are ya doin'? Why are you treating me like shit? Did I get my dick up yer butt?"

Unsure of the answer, Paula considered the question. Why *was* she being so bitchy? Meatboy was just being himself and she didn't really expect much else from him. The glory of the afternoon was fading, a slight chill touched her skin. Paula stepped back into the apartment and closed the patio door halfway.

"I dunno, sorry man. Do you wanna beer?"

"Forget it, I'll get my own beer," said Meatboy storming crossly into the kitchen.

Paula sighed and plopped herself onto the couch. Why did everything have to be so complicated? She turned up the new Snatch Bandits disc. Loud.

I'm feeling good about this day, I'm gonna
buy some beers and make my problems go away.
Then I'll wash it down with some liquor too,
so I think it's about time that I drink with you.

The song only made her guilt worse. She wished she had just gotten him his stupid beer, the crybaby.

In the kitchen Meatboy cracked open a can of Bull Max beer and leaned against the fridge as the sonic wave of punk rock blasted him from the living room. She really had that stereo cranked. Was she trying to tell him something? So maybe he had pushed the *get-me-a-beer* thing a little too far but, he figured, if you could get a girl to bring you a beer in her own place she was putty in your hands. What he needed was something to lighten things up a bit. Meatboy searched the cluttered shelves and cupboards of the small apartment kitchen.

Loading up a well-used soapstone pipe with B.C. bud, Paula brushed aside her regret and flicked a lighter. She hadn't been prepared for Meatboy's sudden visit. He never warned people when he was going to be in town, he just showed up on their doorstep with an armload of booze—or occasionally nothing at all. In a way she was glad to see him; although he was an annoying, drunken asshole, he could also usually be counted on to provide some measure of entertainment. Maybe she had been a little rough on her guest, he had after all, brought a lot of booze. Paula blew out a peppery cloud of smoke and noticed that her own can of beer was almost empty.

"Hey Meatbrain," she yelled over the music. "Bring me a beer!"

No response. Paula put down the pipe and got up from the couch to investigate the kitchen. Over the roar of the tunes Paula heard several metallic clunks. What the hell was he up to in there? Sticking her head into the kitchen, she saw Meatboy leaning against the counter with a beer in one hand, a cagey little smirk on his face.

"What the fuck you up to, you wannabe pirate."

"Nuthin', I'm just chillin' and drinkin'. Seemed like you were kinda steamed so I thought I'd hang here."

Paula didn't trust him one bit. She reached for one of the full cans of beer on the counter,

Meatboy quickly snatched them away. "Nuttin' doing! Get yer own beer!" he nodded towards the fridge.

. Now she really was suspicious. Hesitantly she reached for the fridge handle, pausing to look over at her sneaky guest. He just stood there with a stupid grin on his mug.

"Well go'wan, what'cha waitin' for?" he challenged.

Paula still couldn't figure out what he was up to, but she was getting tired of playing his game. Briskly she yanked open the fridge. The entire door came off in her hand and crashed to the floor with a teeth-shaking KERSMASH! Apple chutney, rancid yellowish marmalade and other largely-ignored, half-finished condiments popped out of the door and shattered explosively on the floor. She let go of the door which, unfettered with hinges, toppled over onto the kitchen table sending breakfast dishes flying in all directions.

"HAW! HAW! HAW!" Meatboy lived for moments like this. He doubled over slapping his thigh and laughed until tears rolled down his face. Taking the hinge pins out of the fridge had been a piece of cake and the expression on Paula's face was priceless.

One look at the sticky mess on her kitchen floor and the red Paula saw wasn't just ketchup. She lost it. "You fucking shitbag! What the hell did you do!" The kitchen looked like it had just scored a direct A-bomb hit. Shattered glassware was strewn to the far corners of the room, and multicoloured jams and sauces were spattered up and down Paula's legs. Scooping up a handful of broken eggs and other gelatinous goop, she whipped the muck at Meatboy's laughing face. Bits of eggshell and chutney stuck to his face and adorned his spiky green hair like semi-edible Christmas tree decorations. The food attack only led her trickster guest to howl even louder.

"HAW! HAW!" roared Meatboy. "You shoulda seen your face!" He slid to his knees, then flopped over onto his side, laughing hysterically. His studded leather vest made a wet sounding crunch against the glass as he rolled around on the floor.

Meatboy was a dead man laughing. Paula jumped on his back and started choking the shit out of him. Her victim continued to guffaw, although with less force.

"Hey!" he sputtered, choking. "Somebody's here!" Meatboy made an effort to point over his shoulder at the door.

"I'm not falling for that one!" said Paula as she continued to throttle him.

"Knock-knock," came a voice from behind them.

Paula released her victim and turned around to face the voice. Her friend Silvi was standing in the doorway looking embarrassed.

"Sorry for barging in. I didn't know you were busy," she paused as she took in the chaos, "but the music was playing and the door was open". She gave up on apologizing and tried to look cool.

Meatboy jumped to his feet wiping fridge goo from his face. "Hey, I'm Meatboy," he said. Realizing his hands were covered with condiments, he wiped them vigorously on his ripped black jeans and extended a sticky hand. Silvi gingerly accepted his grubby mitt and gave it a brief shake.

"I'm Silvi. Sorry to interrupt you guys. I was just passing by and thought I'd drop in for a minute, but you look busy. I should be going." She hitched a small black handbag on her thin shoulder and made leaving motions.

"Nah! Don't worry about it, Sil," said Paula making a superhuman effort to control her fury. "Buttface here was just helping me fix my fridge. Have a beer."

Snagging a Pale Ale from the open fridge, she passed it to Silvi. Noticing that Meatboy was practically drooling on her friend, she kicked him harshly in the shin with her steel cap Daytons. "I said, Meatboy was just fixing the fridge!"

"Yow!" yelped Meatboy grabbing his leg and hopping on the broken glass. He had been so busy checking out the hot-looking arrival he had forgotten all about the fridge and its angry owner. The new girl was a vision in black with blonde trim. He stopped hopping and forgot about cleaning himself.

Paula was still red hot. "Fix that fucking fridge you numbskull!" She pointed to the dismantled appliance.

"Oh yeah," mumbled Meatboy. He was great at taking stuff apart, not so good at putting it back together. Squatting down on his haunches, he examined the situation. It didn't look too bad. If he could just remember where he put those hinge pins.

Meanwhile the girls were doing their best to put the kitchen back in order, Paula still cursing Meatboy under her breath. "That asshole did this just cause I wouldn't get him a beer," she grumbled.

"So who's your friend?" whispered Silvi. "He's kinda cute."

The question caught Paula off guard. She hadn't expected Silvi to be interested in him, and to her greater surprise, she found she was jealous.

"Oh, he's just an old drinkin' buddy. He used to live here but he moved to Toronto to get a band together."

"What, he couldn't do that here?" asked Silvi, lifting an eyebrow.

Paula shrugged. "I think he also had some problems with the cops."

Silvi let the subject drop but continued to watch Meatboy as he wrestled with the fridge.

"Gimme a hand with this thing willya?" he said, struggling with the door. He had found the missing parts but they just didn't seem to fit.

The girls held the door as Meatboy forced the pins into place. Finally the fridge was restored to its former glory and most of the debris had been cleared from the kitchen.

"All done," grinned Meatboy, yanking his arm around to pat himself on the back. He had been worried he wouldn't be able to put the door back on. How would the beer stay cold?

"So what are you guys doing tonight?" asked Silvi. She hadn't come over with any specific plan, but Meatboy was attractive in a Jurassic sort of way. "The Cadillac Tramps are playing at the Commodore."

"Last time I was there, I got in a fight with the bartender," recalled Meatboy. "If he's still working there I won't be able to get in."

"Ah, don't worry about it, he's probably long gone. Bartenders around there usually only last about a week and a half," assured Silvi. She liked it when guys didn't instantly jump to her beck and call.

"I'm kinda broke actually," Paula admitted. "But I like the Tramps."

Meatboy looked at the girls lustfully. He hoped he wouldn't have to pay for both of them, but then again, two birds were better than one.

"So let's go then! I'll buy the tickets and you guys can buy me beer," he offered. Leaving Toronto had been easy after stealing his landlord's income tax refund cheque from the mailbox, and even easier was justifying the theft. Eight hundred and fifty bucks rent for a one-bedroom cockroach-ridden dive in the middle of Cracktown was a total rip off. But the real reason he had left Toronto was because one night at a house party he had stumbled into the wrong room and caught his landlord screwing a German Shepherd. The dog belonged to Meatboy's ex-girlfriend. He had beaten the holy hell out of the dog-raping bastard and the sick fuck had charged him with assault. The mental image of the landlord dripping sweat as he lunged into the dog still haunted him. The worst part of it was the dog seeming to enjoy it. The confused animal was *smiling*. Meatboy shook his head in an attempt to forget.

"What time does the show start?" Paula was in.

"I dunno, the first band usually starts about ten."

"Plenty time for a few beers," Meatboy reasoned.

The CD ended as the trio moved to the living room. Paula found a G.G. Allin and the Murder Junkies disc and slapped it into the deck. She was beginning to defrost a little, but she was still pissed that Silvi was so enamored with that saboteur of a lager lout.

"So did you bring anything with you from Toronto?" she asked conversationally.

Meatboy reached into his leather vest and produced a baggie of white powder. "Just this ounce of dummy dust. Do you guys wanna do some?"

The PCP had also been repo'd from his landlord.

"Stuff that shit!" said Paula. She turned into an earthworm and levitated when she took dummy.

"I might do a couple lines," volunteered Silvi.

Meatboy dug in the bag with the corner of a matchbook cover and plunked several grams of powder on the table. "Go nuts."

"I can't do all this, are you gonna do half?"

"Nah, you go ahead. I don't take that shit."

"If I'm doing some, you're doing some too," stated Silvi matter-of-factly.

"I can't do dummy dust, I always get into fights when I take that stuff," complained Meatboy.

"Well take it back then, I'm not doing any if you're not."

"Ah fuck, just make some rails and I'll try real hard not to get in any trouble."

The PCP was quickly snorted. Paula did consent to a small hit, albeit much less than the huge lines Meatboy and Silvi pigged down. There was a slight moment of silence as the group pondered the fact that for better and probably for worse, their reality would soon be altered. Meatboy was apprehensive. He had a hard time staying out of jail when he took PCP. Things always seemed to start off fine, but suddenly he would be in the middle of some stupid bar brawl. He didn't even particularly like to fight, especially when he was all messed up on drugs. It just happened. He promised himself he would be on his best behavior tonight. Damn, that Silvi was hot! She kept looking at him too. Did that mean something? He also sensed Paula was jealous. Even better.

The PCP was kicking in full force and everyone was feeling fuzzy. Eventually the girls put the final touches on their makeup and Meatboy filled his leather jacket with cans of beer. Even though he had a lot of money and could easily afford to buy beer at the show, he preferred to bring his own. Some habits were hard to break.

"Let's rawk," said Meatboy.

02

The train rolled slowly across the frozen tundra. Inside one of the boxcars three stowaways shivered uncontrollably. In Alberta, spring was still nothing but a dream.

"Quit hoggin' that blanket, ya big lummox!" Tommy punctuated his request with an elbow. "We're cold too, ya know." All three were trying to stay warm under the same thin blanket. Problem was, Atlas was much larger than his companions and consequently needed more of the blanket.

"Why are you always ridin' me, Tommy?" whined the blanket thief. "I didn't do nuthin."

"Would you guys quit bitchin' and moaning?" asked the Rat. "I'm tryin' to get some shut-eye." He pulled his wiry frame into a tighter ball in a futile attempt to stay warm.

Tommy rolled his eyes in disgust. "How the hell can you sleep in this cold? Especially with this guy stealing the blanket!" He jabbed Atlas in the kidney with a stiffened forefinger.

The Rat closed his eyes again. "It'd be easy enough if you guys would just shuddup." He was the older, most experienced of the trio and realized that they should have brought more blankets, but unlike his companions the Rat was pragmatic about the situation. Besides, there wasn't much he could do about it and they would be in Vancouver soon enough.

"Is there anything left to eat?" asked Atlas. "I'm hungry!" He was one of those people who ate non-stop, never exercised, but still managed to look like he had just stepped off the pages of *Fitness Magazine*. It was a trait many people found revolting.

Tommy rolled his eyes again. "You're always hungry! Don't you ever stop eating?"

Atlas didn't answer directly — his feelings were hurt. He got up and moved several yards away from the group. Sitting cross-legged, he stared bitterly at his scuffed combat boots. Without food his social skills fell apart. "I can't help it if I'm hungry," he pouted.

Tommy tried to ignore his large, hungry friend. He sure would hate to be an injured plane crash survivor with that guy around—the thought made him shudder. Wishing he had never let the Rat talk him into leaving Winnipeg, he attempted to shut everything from his mind and go to sleep. After several minutes he gave up. It was impossible to sleep with that big ape just sitting there sulking. He flung off the smelly blanket and got to his feet. Atlas watched as Tommy walked over to the other side of the boxcar and began rummaging through his backpack. Returning with a can of Chef Boyardee Ravioli, he tossed it at his friend's head. Atlas caught the can easily—coordination was not one of his weak points. He smiled appreciatively.

"Gee, thanks, Tommy, thought you were mad at me." He dug out a Swiss army knife from a pocket and attacked the can.

Tommy winced as he watched Atlas rip into the can. He could just imagine him cutting strips of flesh from a dead body with the same willful glee. "I told you not to eat all your food before we even got out of Manitoba," he admonished his friend.

Atlas looked up with a sauce-stained face. "But I was hungry!" He speared another ravioli with his knife.

Tommy shook his head. There was no point in talking to this guy. When it came to food, reason was out the window. I was hungry. Sheeeiit.

The train clattered hypnotically down the tracks as Tommy made his way to the door. Looking out at the passing oil fields, he wondered again if he had made the right decision. Things had really gone to hell after the band had broken up. Just when they had started to make a few bucks, their singer had quit the group to chase a degree in microbiology. The rotten bastard. They had looked around for a new singer but hadn't been able to find anyone with the right stuff. The Rat had some buddies in Vancouver and had been pressuring him and Atlas to move the band to the West Coast. Finally weary of the constant badgering, they had agreed to give it a try. Tommy—who was utterly without income—had been kicked out of his apartment and was reduced to sleeping on his friends' couches. That was definitely no way for a rock star to live. "Welfare is easy to collect in B.C.," the Rat had told them. Tommy sure hoped so. None of them had even been able to raise enough money to take the bus to Vancouver. Once again, the Rat had an answer. "We can hop a freight train. I've done it before, there's nothing to it."

It wasn't so bad actually, and if they had just brought enough food and warm clothing they might even be comfortable. Tommy knew it was his nature to worry too much, but he felt this time he had valid reasons for being apprehensive. For one, the Rat had stopped short of saying they actually had a place to stay when they got to Vancouver—their next address could be under a bridge for all he knew. Again, hardly suitable digs for The Next Big Thing. Atlas didn't seem worried though, he had finished the can of ravioli and was noisily scraping the sides of the tin with his knife. All that gorilla cared about was where his next meal was coming from. Simple bugger didn't even drink or take drugs. Sometimes Tommy envied the big guy.

"Hey Tommy," said Atlas from his seat on the floor. "What does N.T.R.A. mean?"

Distracted from his brooding, Tommy turned to the massive guitarist. "Huh? What you talking 'bout?" He walked over to see what Atlas was looking at. On the wall of the boxcar someone had scrawled N.T.R.A. in bold felt pen. Underneath was a crudely fashioned skull and railway spikes.

"Beats me," said Tommy scratching his head. "Must be some kind of gang." He was familiar with tagging. Winnipeg had become overrun with gangs in the nineties—yet another good reason to leave town.

Atlas shrugged. Gangs were of little interest to him. He turned his attention back to the empty can and saw with pleasure that minute particles still clung to the sides.

The Rat stirred in his sleep. The solemn drummer could sleep through anything — once he had slept through a police raid. When he woke up the cops had carted everybody off to jail but had completely overlooked him sleeping under a pile of rags, a half ounce of Afganny hash in his pants pocket. Sleeping was his favorite hobby.

The train began to lose speed, almost imperceptibly at first then more noticeably as the conductor applied the brakes. The shrill sound of metal on metal cut through the car like a cat in a blender.

"Shit!" said Tommy going back to the door. "What the fuck is going on?" Grain elevators and farm buildings appeared. In the distance a handful of tall buildings poked out of the flat, rural landscape. They seemed to be approaching civilization of some kind. "What place is this?" He had never seen the prairies, let alone from a boxcar.

Atlas came to the door and gazed out. "Looks like Edmonton," he said, throwing the ravioli can into the ditch.

Tommy threw him a curious look. "How the fuck would you know?"

"Seen pictures of it in a book," replied the king-sized guitarist licking his lips. He went over to his pack and began digging through it again. "I must have something left to eat!" Discovering a Crunchie bar, he tore hungrily at the wrapper.

Tommy gave his companion a curious look. Every time he was convinced Atlas was submoronic, the big guy would throw him a curve ball. He turned to watch the approaching city. "I hope we're not going to stop. What if they decide to load up this car?" Atlas, though, was more concerned that a crumb from his chocolate bar might escape consumption.

In a corner the Rat farted loudly. The noise or the smell must have woke him. He sat up slowly and rubbed his eyes.

"Phew! Who died? Hey, why are we stopping? Where are we?" He quickly regained his street composure and focused. The Rat was the only one of the group who had truly been born deprived; his smarts were born of sheer necessity. As a youth he had been teased for his sharp features and pointy nose and had to learn to fight. When he was thirteen he was sent to the juvenile detention center for stabbing his richly deserving stepfather. Given the opportunity, he would stab that grouchy old son-of-a-bitch again. Punk music focused his anger and gave him a voice—he felt wild joy at being able to release his pent-up frustrations. He had power. Freedom.

"Move those packs into the corner behind that pile of junk," he ordered. They had to be ready for a possible search. He picked up his own pack and moved it behind a pallet of greasy train wheels.

Atlas and Tommy followed the Rat's command without question. It was smarter just to listen than it was to apologize later. Even after the trio had stashed their things as well as possible, there were no hiding spots that would hold up beyond a quick examination. Without a cargo manifest, there was no way to tell whether the boxcar you jumped into contained either toxic waste or other freeloaders; while at the same time, breaking a lock and seal meant almost certain discovery. The idea was to pick a recently unloaded car and hope to avoid detection.

The train continued to slow, cutting through the evening air like fingernails on a blackboard. The Rat took a last look out the door. A blood-red sunset stained the horizon and fat purple clouds loitered threateningly. A moist heaviness in the air promised rain. Shivering, he slammed the door hard, but it bounced back and remained open several inches. The locking mechanism was jammed. The Rat frowned; an open car was much more likely to be searched by the c.p. police, who were a separate law unto themselves.

"Maybe we should get off here," suggested Atlas. Any change was okay with him. Besides, there had to be a fast-food restaurant around here somewhere.

"Yeah man, great idea. These hicks would love you," observed Tommy. His bandmate was constantly infuriating people beyond the point of reason just with his outrageous size and appearance. At six-foot-six, and two hundred and fifty-two pounds of cartoon tattoos and razor-sharp, studded black leather punk accessories, the guitarist was every mother's nightmare. But like many giants, Atlas was essentially a sensitive gentleman who avoided violence. He could never understand why he was so often treated like Frankenstein.

"Get over here, you fuck-up," said Tommy. He and the Rat had already found themselves semi-comfortable positions behind a pile of scrap iron and were as hidden from sight as they could be. Atlas came over and squeezed his massive frame into the tiny spot his mates had reserved for him. As he struggled to make himself comfortable, the locomotive came to a complete stop, starting a chain reaction of loud, jarring collisions.

"Jesus! What a racket!" exclaimed Atlas as the train shook violently. This from a guy who thought nothing of standing in front of a stack of Marshall amplifiers all night.

"Shhh," whispered Tommy and the Rat. Someone was walking down the row of boxcars banging on the doors with a heavy baton. The footsteps stopped outside and paused, a hand wrenching open the door with a rusty squeal. The stowaways tried to make themselves invisible as scrutinizing eyes swept past them. After what seemed like an eternity, the door banged and the crunch of footsteps on gravel went on to the next car.

"Man! that was close!" said Atlas.

"SHHHH!" repeated his mates.

A light patter of rain began to hit the roof of the box-car, the sound magnified and echoing in the stillness. The trio waited in silence.

Atlas could remain quiet no longer. "How long are we going to be stuck here?" he asked.

Tommy shot him an exasperated look. "How the hell should we know?"

The Rat made no comment. He was used to waiting; patience was his virtue. Producing a small folding knife, he began fastidiously cleaning his nails. Tommy got up and lit the Coleman lamp they had fortunately remembered to bring. It was already dark.

"Maybe we should get out, and see if we can find another train headed west," he suggested. He was tired of waiting.

"Just relax," said the Rat without looking up from his fingernails. "We'll be moving soon."

It began raining in earnest. Falling in sheets, the sound of water hitting the tin roof was deafening. A flash of lightning turned darkness to daylight. Seconds later heavy thunder followed like an angry god pounding the earth. Atlas stayed crouched in the corner and tried not to show his fear. Thunder scared him.

Tommy went over and closed the door as best he could. It occurred to him that the faulty latch may have been the reason the car had not been loaded with valuable goods. Suddenly the train lurched into motion, nearly knocking the startled bassist to his feet.

"Yay!" cheered Atlas happily. Overcoming his fear of the storm, he unfolded himself from his cramped quarters and began searching his pack for any bits of food he might have overlooked.

The train began to pick up speed. Suddenly the door slid back on its rollers and two cloth packs were pitched into the boxcar. Moments later, two dark figures clambered aboard. A brilliant flash of lightning illuminated the new arrivals. A wicked scar ran vertically across the first guest's face, bisecting his left eye. His smile revealed badly rotting teeth.

"Well, well, Otis. It looks like we got us some riding companions!"

Otis was slightly smaller than his friend but equally gruesome-looking. He glanced at Tommy and Atlas. "They look like a couple of freaks."

"Now Otis," said the first hobo. "That wasn't a very polite thing to say, I'm sure these boys aren't freaks at all. We probably just need to get to know each other a little better." He flashed the rotten grin and held a gnarled hand out to Tommy. "My name is Earl, and this," he said jerking a thumb at his companion, "in case you hadn't already guessed, is Otis."

03

Onstage at the Commodore Ballroom, the Cadillac Tramps were putting the crowd through its paces. The dance floor was the place to be if you liked things hot, loud, and sweaty. Intent on maximizing the impact, the Tramps would slow down just enough to let the crowd catch its collective breath before piling into the next song at two hundred miles an hour. The suspended dance floor bounced like a gas-powered trampoline.

Gabby, the group's pot-bellied singer, ignored the gallons of beer splashed on him by the crowd and threw himself into the mosh pit with little regard for life or limb. The slam-dancers had no intention of letting the portly singer hit the floor—if he was injured, the show would come to an abrupt end. Catching the sweaty frontman mid-air, the fans carried him across the dance floor to the bar where many drinks waited. Not willing to offend the fans with his sobriety, Gabby up-ended glass after glass into his open mouth but allowed the suds to spill out. Excess beer splashed everywhere. Unaware of the singer's chicanery, the enthusiastic fans carried Gabby back across the dance floor and tossed him back on the stage.

Meatboy was rawkin' up a storm. Arms and legs akimbo, he kept his head down and skanked for freedom. Risking mortal injury, he snuck a glance at the girls to see if they were watching him. Paula and Silvi stood at the edge of the dance floor bopping their heads in time to the music. To his chagrin, neither was paying him the slightest bit of attention. Put off by this lack of worship, he failed to notice a stage-diver flying directly towards him. It wasn't until the last instant he became aware of the danger and threw up an arm to deflect the human projectile. It was futile. The airborne suburban teenager landed directly on top of him like a concrete block off the freeway overpass. Skull met skull as both diver and dancer went down to the floor in a tangle of arms and legs. As usual, the flyer was relatively unharmed and bounced to his feet rubbing his head. Meatboy lay prone on the floor, unconscious.

Coming to his aid, several slam-dancers picked Meatboy up and moved him to safety away from the dance floor. One mohawked punk checked his vital signs and made sure he was still breathing. Satisfied that his patient was only knocked out, the punk left to rejoin his friends in the pit. Meatboy, still prone, was far away, drifting.

"Eat your cauliflower Terry, it's getting cold!" His mother trilled at him across the supper table. Terry looked at the disgusting-looking white clumps on his plate and made mock vomiting noises.

"None of that at the table!" roared his father turning red. "Now eat your supper!"

Terry reluctantly pried a small morsel of cauliflower away from the main clump and placed it tentatively on his tongue. He bit into the vegetable and chewed it twice before spitting the revolting mess back onto his plate "Yuck! This tastes gross! I want some more meat!"

His father jumped to his feet, chair flying over backwards. Racing around the table, he seized Terry by the collar and propelled him backwards into the wall. "Meat?" he cried. "All you ever want is meat! You're nothing but a little Meatboy! Just eat your cauliflower, and grow up!"

Young Meatboy began to wail. "But I don't wanna—!"

"I don't wanna grow up!" he shouted. His eyes began to focus and he could see Paula and Silvi hovering overhead, viewing him with concern.

"It's okay, Meatboy. You don't have to grow up," Paula assured him calmly. "C'mon, get up. It's time to go."

"Huh? Where are we?" slurred Meatboy, still dazed.

"We're at the Commodore. You had a little accident. The staff wanted to call an ambulance, but I knew you had that PCP on you, and talked them out of it." She was relieved that Meatboy had regained consciousness. He had been out cold for half an hour. The band was packing up their gear, and the staff were waiting impatiently; everybody wanted to go home.

Meatboy sat up and gingerly touched the back of his head. Electrical bolts of pain shot from a golf-ball sized lump. Quickly, he withdrew his hand. Stupid PCP always got him into fights. "How's the other guy?" he asked hopefully, "Is he in the hospital?"

"You didn't get in a fight, silly," Paula told him, "A stage diver landed on you."

"A stage diver?" said Meatboy incredulously. "Shit, I missed the band cause of him!" Getting slowly to his feet, he checked his pockets to see if he still had all his stuff. Beer? Check. Money? Check. Dope? Check. Cigarettes? Nope. Oh well, three out of four wasn't bad. Suddenly he realized that he could use this injury for a little sympathy. "Gimme a hand girls, I'm feelin' a little dizzy." He half-feigned a sway.

Paula and Silvi rushed to support him, one on each side. Meatboy gratefully put his arms around his female rescuers. They were so soft and pretty smelling. This was worth being maimed. The trio limped slowly from the hall.

"What are we gonna do now?" asked Meatboy. He was starting to feel a lot better—even the dummy dust was wearing off a little.

"Don't you wanna go somewhere and rest?" asked Silvi. "You might have a concussion."

Still feeling hazy, it never occurred to Meatboy that Silvi might be inviting him back to her place—besides he wanted to party. "Nah, I'm fine. Isn't there any after-hours joints we can go to?"

Silvi was buzzed and wanted to fuck Meatboy, but she wasn't going to hand it to him on a silver platter. She glanced at Paula, who returned the look with one of sheer bitchiness. Ahh, the hell with her.

"There's a punk booze can down on Clark that's probably open." Silvi volunteered. She liked the way the new guy could take a lump.

"Cool! Let's get a cab." Meatboy stepped to the curb under his own power; and putting his fingers to his lips, he let out a piercing whistle. A shiny new Chrysler taxi cut across three lanes of traffic and slid smoothly to the curb. With a rare gesture of gallantry, Meatboy opened the rear door for the girls. Paula hesitated. She could see Silvi intended to move in on her guest—not that she really cared—but she wasn't interested in being a third wheel. Against her better judgment, she got into the cab.

"Take us to the booze can on Clark," Silvi told the driver. She didn't know the exact address but it was around there somewhere. The driver nodded knowingly. He was familiar with the after-hours club and its punk patrons—and as distasteful as he found them, he was glad to take their money. He pulled smartly into traffic.

Silvi had noticed Paula's indecision and wanted to get things out in the open. She was tired of trying to guess what her friend was thinking.

"What's up Paula? Are you mad at me or something? What's going on?"

"Naw, I'm not mad at you." She looked to the front seat to see if Meatboy was listening. Despite the cabbie's objections, her house pest had produced an Accused tape and slapped it into the deck. Raucous punk-metal filled the car. "But I just wish you'd checked with me before moving in on Meatboy."

"I *did* check with you!" Silvi said hotly. "You didn't seem to give a damn back at your place." She crossed her legs and steamed.

Paula was silent. She hadn't cared about Meatboy until Silvi had shown interest—actually she had wanted to kill him. Silvi, with her leggy, blonde looks, always got her pick of the guys. So why was she after Meatboy? But looking out the window, she had to admit that her friend was right. Maybe it was her life that was bothering her. Since she had moved out of her ex-boyfriend's house, it had been one long uphill battle to find and maintain a job that paid well enough to keep the roof over her head. Right now, she was working as a junior travel agent, and at ten bucks an hour, it was just barely enough to get by on. Oh, stupid world.

Silvi glared at her friend. What was eating her? With her dark, good looks and quick, sexy smile, Paula could have any guy she wanted so what did she care about one smelly old punk rocker? Come to think of it, what did she want with Meatboy? She glanced at the passenger in the front seat just to make sure her instinct had been correct. He did have a certain animal appeal that had been sorely missing in her last two boyfriends—they had both been absorbed in making money and driving sweet cars. He looked like he might be good and wild in bed, if you could get him there.

Hanging his arm out the window, Meatboy kept furious time to the music by beating on the door panel. Oblivious to the conflict in the back seat, his thoughts became more lucid as he pondered his next move. If there was a Canada-wide warrant out for his arrest, he would be picked up when he tried to apply for welfare. He didn't mind working but he had a hard time finding jobs. Maybe it was the FUCK tattooed on his right knuckles and the YOU on his left that made prospective employers wary. Either way he had to do something. He had only three hundred dollars left, which might well be spent before the night was through. He could only hope to offload his PCP on Vancouver's punk scene.

Sneaking a peek at the girls in the rearview mirror, he gave them a quick male appraisal. There was no question of Silvi's beauty—she was a knock-out. Problem was she looked a bit too spoiled, a bit too clean for his taste. Now Paula he really liked. She was a die-hard punker who didn't take shit from nobody. And sexy? Gawdamn! Unfortunately, it seemed Paula didn't feel the same way about him. Maybe he could convince her he wasn't such a bad guy after all, but for now he wasn't going to worry about it. These things had a way of working themselves out.

"Clark and Vernon," announced the cab driver. He was glad to be rid of his noisy passengers. But would they pay him?

Meatboy recovered his tape from the deck and tossed some bills at the driver. "Here, get yourself some new tapes." He always overtipped; money went through his hands like shit through a goose. Disgorged of its contents, the cab raced off into the night.

"So where the hell is this booze can?" asked Meatboy, cracking a warm beer.

Silvi looked around at the run-down neighborhood and shivered. It sure would suck to live down here — then again, Meatboy probably lived in a neighborhood like this and she was glad he was along to provide protection. "This way," she said pointing down the street.

Meatboy took several steps, then stopped. He had forgotten his sympathy crutches. "I'm starting to get dizzy again, girls," he said holding his head with one hand and staggering theatrically.

Paula and Silvi each took an arm. They weren't fooled by Meatboy's act but decided to go along with it just to keep him from whining. The trio wobbled/stumbled on down the street.

"So what's this place called?" wondered Meatboy. With an arm around each girl, it was hard to drink. He loosened his grip on Silvi and took a long slug.

"THE WHAT," answered Silvi.

"No, what's this place called?"

"THE WHAT."

"What?" Meatboy wondered if he was still zonked on the dummy dust.

"The booze can is called THE WHAT," Paula said condescendingly.

Finally Meatboy understood. With a straight face he turned to her and asked, "So, who's on second?" He knew his Abbot and Costello.

Both girls gave him the ol' fish-eye. Crickets were chirping.

"Aw c'mon girls, gimme a break. I don't get paid for this!"

"Good thing," Paula observed dryly.

Down a back alley, muffled, high-density punk rock was pounding from one of the warehouses that littered the area. Silvi walked up to a blue door and pounded loudly. A dead-bolt was unlocked and the door flung open. The bouncer was a tall, lanky freak who was bald but for a shock of bright red hair in the center of his forehead. He eyeballed the girls lustily. "C'mon in! Four bucks each, comes to nine bucks total." Hormones had adversely affected his math.

Meatboy gave him fifteen. "Get yourself some more hair dye," he mumbled. It was hard for him to come up with zingers for everyone he tipped.

The doorman completely missed the barb thrown in his direction. He was too busy trying to chat up the girls. "So what's yer names?" He ignored Meatboy and leered drunkenly at the female guests.

Paula and Silvi didn't think an effort this lame deserved recognition; they grabbed Meatboy by the arms and steered him into the club. Inside the ware-house it was hot, dark, smoky, and oddly, smelled of Vic's Vapour Rub.

"Where's the bar?" roared Meatboy over the death-cookie band onstage. A banner behind the thundering roar read "TUMULT". They were.

"This way!" yelled Silvi tugging on his sleeve. She didn't really care for ear-shattering music but she liked the wild crowds it attracted. She pushed her way through the crowd to the bar, which was in an adjoining room at the back.

Paula scowled but decided to give Silvi a clear shot at the dubious object of her affection. Looking around the smoky club she spotted some members of a local punk band sitting at a table drinking. She made her way over and pulled out a chair.

"Anyone sittin' here, Noel?" she asked the crusty-looking lead singer.

Noel took a large swill of beer before replying. "You are sweetheart, park it." He turned his attention back to the conversation with his mates.

Paula sighed and lit a cigarette. All the band members appeared to have dates, and all were pissed to the gills. She got up again and made her way slowly to the bar, stopping to yell with friends and acquaintances along the way.

The packed bar was a world unto itself. Besides the punkers, a typical Saturday morning saw plenty of business from skaters, outlaw bikers, gangbangers, and longshoremen, jammed together, elbow to elbow. As Paula plunged into the haze of murky beerness, the first thing she saw was Meatboy standing center stage at the bar, a huge pile of dummy dust in front of him. Gregariously, he offered free lines to one and all. Silvi hung giggling from his arm. The little tramp.

Pushing her way through the crowd, Paula sidled up next to Meatboy. "What the hell are you doing? I thought you were going to sell this shit!" Meatboy would become a burden if he had no money.

Meatboy looked at her blankly. "Aaargghh! Blah blot zug?" he garbled. Clearly he'd been sampling his own wares. Disgusted, Paula looked to Silvi for help. Silvi was still giggling and her eyes were shiny with the drug. She always giggled when she was too stoned to talk.

"Ahh, Jesus!" said Paula throwing up her hands in frustration. "You idiots can just fucking rot, I'm going home!" She turned on one heel and stomped from the bar.

"Whadda hell's wrong wid her?" slurred Meatboy to no one in particular.

Silvi looked at him with zonked eyes and made an effort to speak coherently. "Where Paulo go..." Her grip on Meatboy's arm was partly to remain upright.

Her blitzed benefactor scraped out more rough lines. "Everybody have anudder!" he bellowed. A longshoreman on his left quickly dipped his head and two large rails disappeared.

"More beer!" shouted Meatboy throwing money on the bar.

Greg, the bartender, could see problems. He leaned across the bar. "Listen, I want you to put that fuckin' shit away right fuckin' now." He was a scrawny little guy but was not to be trifled with. He kept a sawed-off baseball bat under the bar and knew how to use it.

"Gimme anudder beer!" demanded Meatboy.

"Don't say I didn't warn you," said Greg. And with that, he swept the pile of PCP off the bar onto the beer-soaked floor. "You're cut off," he said, adding insult to injury.

"Aaaarrrgghhh!" bellowed Meatboy reaching for the bartender's neck. It was a futile gesture. With a minimum of fuss, he was quickly pummeled into submission by the bar staff and tossed into the alley.

Outside, Meatboy beat on the door in frustration. "Gimme back my goil!" he yelled impotently.

"Piss off!" came a voice from inside the club.

Eventually Meatboy wore out his fists and stumbled dejectedly away from the booze can. A slight rain began to fall, further dampening his spirits. At Hastings St. he looked around for a cab that would take him back to Paula's. He hoped she'd let him back in—she had seemed pretty pissed off for some reason. With no taxis in sight, he continued to trudge slowly in what he hoped was the right direction. The PCP was making it difficult to walk, so he reached into his jacket and pulled out a can of warm beer. At least he hadn't gotten into any fights. Looking around for familiar landmarks and not seeing any, he conceded that he was probably lost. No matter. If he kept walking he was bound to recognize something.

A green Ford pickup truck barreled towards him as he crossed a street. Jumping back to avoid being hit, Meatboy flashed the reckless driver double digits. Stupid move. The truck hammered on its brakes and skidded to a smoky halt.

Oh fuck, thought Meatboy, here we go again. He was too wasted to fight, it might be better to take it on the lam. With all the speed he could muster, he began lumbering towards a nearby park.

"Get that punk rock faggot!" came a shout from behind him. Couldn't these rednecks come up with anything a little more original? Heavy bootsteps slapped on concrete behind Meatboy as he headed into the park. Already he was winded — his leather jacket was heavy even when it was empty, and he still had about three beers left in it. A sudden stubbornness reared its head. Stopping in his tracks, Meatboy whipped off his quick-release chain belt and turned to face his attackers. Somebody was gonna get fucked up.

The three drunk rednecks paused slightly when they saw the punker swinging the chain, but not for long. Crazed with beer and testosterone, they piled on their victim with irrational fury. Meatboy never had a chance. The first and only swing of his belt tore across one assailant's face, ripping acne-pocked flesh. Then he was buried. Fists, bottles, and boots rained down on him in a blinding barrage of pain. After a while he stopped caring, and only the occasional flash of white light reminded him he was still being beaten. Eventually it was over. One of his attackers, a tall, skinny loogan with long greasy hair and a filthy 'Playland' cap, bent over and spat in his bloody face. "See ya later, faggot!" he said applying a final brutal kick to the ribcage.

Mercifully, Meatboy lost consciousness. The rain came down harder and washed the blood into a pink halo around his head.

04

The Rat was naturally paranoid, and with his built in instinct he could tell these guys were definitely bad news. He watched the strangers and fingered the knife in his jacket pocket

Atlas was much more open and naive. He thought Earl's scar was pretty cool. "Hey! I'm Atlas," he said crushing the stranger's hand with unconscious, good-willed strength.

"You sure are," winced Earl retrieving his damaged hand. His bones were brittle and arthritic from decades of rail riding and hard drinking.

Otis pulled a bottle of Ginseng brandy from his pack and took a conservative tug. He glanced at his partner with one good eye—the other was made of glass. It was great to be moving again. Hefting the jug with the skill of a butcher, Earl took the punkers in with a calculating, predatory look. He drank deeply. "So what is it you boys are doin' out here in the middle of nowhere?" he asked wiping a grey-whiskered mouth with the back of his hand.

Tommy didn't figure it was anybody's business but his own. "Bird watching," he said tightly.

Earl ignored Tommy's glib reply and turned his attention to the largest, most potentially dangerous of the trio. The big freak looked strong enough to crush rocks, but not much smarter than one. It was the quiet, dark one in the corner trimming his fingernails with an evil-looking knife that made him cautious. Ever the opportunist, he looked for a simple, practical way to relieve his fellow wanderers of any valuable items.

"Gotta smoke?" he said, turning to Atlas. It was a quick way to gain psychological advantage.

Atlas patted the pockets of his studded leather jacket apologetically. "Sorry man, I don't smoke."

"Well, what *do* you have? You big fuckin' moron." This kind of behavior was typical for Otis when meeting strangers on trains. He wasted little time picking fights. Taking a step back, he slipped a hand into his tattered green parka.

Atlas was confused. He naturally assumed that anyone they met on this big adventure would be as friendly as he was. The old guy seemed alright, but the short, mean-looking one was clearly looking for trouble. Besides, the word 'moron' struck a sensitive nerve. His anger moved in like a summer storm. "Who you callin' moron? Shorty!" His hands balled up into heavy bludgeons.

Tommy could see things were going to get worse before they got better. He knew his friend could lick almost anybody as long as it was a one-on-one fight. If the old guy tried to jump in, Tommy planned to kick his head clean off. Unsurprisingly, Atlas's foe yanked a gun from his jacket.

"Who you callin' shorty? Fuckface," growled Otis thumbing back the hammer of his pistol. At the same instant, and quick as lightning, Earl's fist streaked out and connected solidly with Tommy's temple. He fell unconscious to the deck. When he woke up, Atlas was shaking him gently, a concerned look on his face. "Wake up, Tommy! Wake up!"

Looking around groggily, Tommy noticed his friends were the only remaining occupants of the boxcar. "Wha' happened? Where are those assholes?" He was missing bits of the picture.

Atlas was his usual articulate self. "That guy was gonna shoot me! A-a-nd then the Rat threw his knife at him and he fell down!" His face was flushed with exertion and Tommy saw he had blood on his hands.

"Then what happened?" He knew there was more.

"Then Atlas threw them off the train," said the Rat, unruffled and putting away his knife.

"Off?" Judging from the sound of the clickety-clack, the train was moving at a pretty good clip. Not that Tommy was worried about the fate of the would-be ex-bullies, but still...

"That guy punched you!" said Atlas hoping Tommy would understand. "I got mad!"

The Rat cracked an uncharacteristic grin. "Yeah, you sure did," he said clapping a hand on his friend's huge, shaking shoulder.

"What about the gun? How bad were they hurt?" Tommy's head was spinning and a large welt was growing on his left temple.

Atlas started to reply, but the Rat cut him off. "After the first guy went down with my knife in him, Atlas grabbed the other guy and slammed him into the door real hard. Then he opened the door and we threw those bums out, the gun too. The guy I stabbed was in too much pain to put up much of a fight, the other one was out cold. They'll probably be alright, I only got the dude in the shoulder. They might be a bit fucked up from bouncing in the ditch though." The Rat clammed up and rolled a smoke from a package of Drum tobacco.

"You okay, Tommy?" Atlas asked worriedly.

"Yeah, I'm fine man, thanks." Tommy got to his feet and took a tour of the boxcar. He stopped and nudged the hobo's abandoned packs with his foot. "Hey, you forgot to toss this shit out." With an angry foot, he started to kick the rucksacks into flying history.

"Wait!" shouted Atlas. "They might have something to eat in there!" He seized one of the grimy packs and shook for food.

"What could those bums possibly have that we might need?" asked Tommy quite reasonably.

Atlas looked at him like he had antlers. "Even bums have to eat!" Opening the pack, he dumped the contents onto the floor of the boxcar. Dirty rags of clothing, a dented aluminum frying pan, and other assorted odds and ends added up to absolutely zero. Looking disappointed, Atlas rooted through the trash. "Can you believe this?" he complained. "That guy had nuthin'!"

"What did you expect?" said the Rat, "Priceless Inca gold? The Mona Lisa? A Big Mac maybe."

"I need something to eat!" bellowed Atlas. Betrayed, his stomach now started to gnaw painfully at his innards. He weakly continued the search until he found something that caught his attention. "Check this out," he said holding up a large, folding knife.

"Let's see that," said Tommy.

Atlas handed it over. He obeyed his pal without question and trusted him implicitly. Tommy studied the knife. "Uh-oh," he said. "Look at this." The initials N.T.R.A. were burned into the wooden haft.

"Those clowns probably belong to some kind of gang," said the Rat, stating the obvious. His mates had already beat him to the same conclusion.

"Big deal," said Tommy unconvincingly. "Maybe those guys were the only members. Besides, there's no way those jerks could have gotten back on the train, we were going way too fast." Tommy was worried, but didn't want his apprehension to show.

Meanwhile Atlas was singlemindedly searching for grub. His desperation paid off. "Look what I found!" he said excitedly holding up a big package of beef jerky. He tore open the bag and began stuffing his face with large strips of the dried beef without waiting for a reaction from his mates, To his satisfaction, his pals appeared uninterested in his bounty.

"That shit is gonna make you thirsty," warned Tommy. There was nothing to drink on board—water was another of the many essential items the boys had neglected to bring.

"Who cares?" said Atlas with his mouth full. He wolfed down the ejected hobo's bag of snacks with gusto. Finishing, he tossed the empty bag aside and belched resoundingly. "I'm thirsty," he complained. "Got anything to drink?"

The matter of the monogrammed knife had already been forgotten by everyone except Tommy. "Drink my piss," he said. "I warned you."

The train rolled on in the dark. The three stowaways fell silent, each immersed in their own world. Atlas was still thirsty, but he was not a frail creature by any means. Once he realized there was nothing else to eat or drink, he put the matter out of his mind. One thing Atlas liked about himself was that he could stay amused for hours on end simply by thinking about the past. Putting himself into a trance-like state, he floated off into the relative peace of his childhood:

"Billy, come in the house. All your guests are waiting for you!" Billy was annoyed, and he looked towards the house with a frown. His tree fort was just starting to come together—

he didn't have time for a stupid birthday party. Selecting a choice piece of lumber from a stack of scraps on the lawn, he set it on his work bench and began pulling out the rusty nails. His mother must have heard the sound of ongoing construction. She screamed at him through the screen door.

"Biiilllllly! Get in here, your guests are waiting!"

"I'm busy, have the party without me!" he yelled. Normally he wouldn't mind but this was the worst possible timing. He was preparing to climb up the tree where his fort awaited when the standard threat came back to him.

"If I have to call your father you're going to be sorry!"

Billy hesitated; his dad was kind of scary. Buckling under the pressure, he chucked the scrap of wood to the ground. You could never win with his parents. Brushing dirt and sawdust from his clothing, he left his work behind and entered the kitchen through the back door.

"SURPRISE!" hollered the assembled guests gathered in the kitchen. Ten red candles burned atop a large, chocolate cake.

'Some surprise', thought Billy. He had known about the party for weeks, and it wasn't like anybody had ever tried to keep it a secret. All the neighborhood kids were waiting impatiently for him to blow out the candles so they could eat the cake. Billy relaxed — the cake did look pretty good. Letting out a mighty gust of wind, he extinguished the candles. Even at his young age, his height and weight was prodigious. His classmates called him 'Kong'.

"Yay!" clapped his best friend Tommy. He was the only one of the guests Billy actually liked. The rest were too normal. In fact, everything was too normal and boring. Billy promised himself, not for the first time, that when he grew up he would do something that was not boring. Something wild.

The cake was rapidly cut and consumed, his mother hovering nearby with a smile of maternal pride. The guests moved to an *adjoining room where a modest pile of birthday presents awaited. Sated with cake, Billy ripped into the gifts. Most of the gifts were sweaters and socks, as he suspected. Just what he always wanted, but not very much. One large present did intrigue him though, and it was this he saved for last.*

"Open that one now, Billy!" pointed Tommy at the oddly-shaped gift.

Billy opened the package carefully. It was suspiciously light, and felt fragile. A card on the gift read, To Billy: with love from Mom and Dad. There was something different about this one, and he intuitively knew this gift would change his life forever. As he peeled away the final wrappers he saw the guitar underneath, a joyous feeling tugged at his young heart. It was the most beautiful thing he had ever seen.

"Cool!" said little Tommy.

An empty orange-juice bottle rolled slowly from one end of the boxcar to the other. The train was climbing a hill. Quick as a shot, the Rat grabbed the Coleman lamp and suspended it on a wire hanging from the roof of the boxcar. Up and up they went, farther into the night. Tommy, who had been slumbering against the wall, fell over onto his side. Startled, he awoke. In his dream, he had been onstage at CBGB's cranking out high-decibel punk rock before hordes of adoring fans—a far cry from rolling along hungry in a frigid, old train.

"Whuzzup? Where are we?" Not for the first time that day, he was completely disoriented.

"We must be near Jasper," said Atlas. His companions gave him a strange look. He seemed to know a lot about geography for someone who had never been out of Manitoba. The Rat got up and opened the door of the boxcar. Outside, it was darker than a politician's soul.

The Rat sensed a great vastness, as if the train was flying through space. Picking up the juice bottle which had rolled back towards him, he tossed it out the door. It vanished without a sound—there was nothing below them but dark.

"What time is it?" asked Atlas.

They gave him another strange look. "Who the fuck cares?" said Tommy. "What difference does it make?"

"I was just wondering," pouted Atlas. "You didn't have to bite my head off." His stomach was wondering how long the trip would last, and when they would arrive in Vancouver.

Tommy got up and sat next to Atlas. "Don't worry, big guy. We'll be in Vancouver soon, and when we do we'll go to the first restaurant we see and eat everything on the menu twice." He knew his jumbo-sized companion was thinking about food.

Atlas seemed consoled by the idea and curled up on the floor of the boxcar. Tommy threw the sole blanket over his hungry friend. Unknown to them, they were already well into British Columbia. The train rolled on.

Earl and Otis staggered down the railway tracks. Otis was clutching his shoulder and moaning softly. He was a big baby when the tables were turned. "That fuckin' punk rocker *stabbed* me!" he whined. Blood had leaked down the inside of his parka and congealed in his underwear. His wound hurt but he wasn't going to die.

"Aw shaddap, ya dang sissy. You shoulda shot that big ape when ya had the chance. I think the gorilla broke me!" For emphasis, Earl rubbed the small of his back with a horny hand and limped exaggeratedly.

This mishap was only the latest in a streak of bad luck that had begun in Missouri. First they almost drowned in a flash flood on the prairies—Otis looked so funny when he was trying to swim. Then an overzealous train cop had rousted them from an A+ ride in an empty passenger car. To top things off, Earl had lost a boot in the mud during their escape, and they had had to rob an unaffiliated rail bum for his boots. Sometimes being a rail-riding, ass-whuppin' bad guy was really a stick in the throat.

"Who are you callin' sissy? It ain't my fault you got hurt," Otis said defensively. He and Earl had never really figured out who was leader, and who was follower. Both were good at giving orders, but were poor at taking them. The only thing they did agree on was that all booze should be shared equally, and that they should get as much of it as possible. Whether they liked it or not, they made a good robbin' and drinkin' team. Earl grimaced under his whiskers—his neck really did hurt. He couldn't tell what he hated most, his partner's constant bellyaching or his new boots fitting so poorly that he felt his feet had been dipped in hydrochloric acid. He was about to punch Otis in the head when he heard a lonesome whistle blow.

"Maybe our ride's a comin'," said Earl. In the darkness there was no way to tell how far away the train was or which direction it was coming from.

Otis, the expert trainspotter of the two, stopped and cocked an ear. "It's coming from the east but it's moving too fast, we'll never make it."

Naturally Earl wouldn't accept this, and was ready to prove Otis wrong. "Bullshit," he said. "We're catching this train." But for the life of him, he couldn't figure out how.

"You sure as shit ain't Superman, you can't stop that train," said Otis. It was a cold, hard fact.

Earl would rather be a sorcerer than a superhero. He checked his pockets for some magic to slow the train but all he could find was a disposable lighter and a half bag of stale peanuts. The train was fast approaching, closing in like an angry bear. Otis stumbled over an old railway tie and pitched forwards, yelping in pain. He had been holding his pierced shoulder with his good arm, and had no way to prevent himself from doing a lip stand on the loose gravel. Earl made a sound like a bucket of rocks being poured on a tin roof. He was laughing.

"Stop laughing, you drunk fuckin' asshole, I'm hurt bad!" cried Otis. The only thing worse than being hurt was to having someone laugh at you when you're down. Earl did stop laughing, but only because he was busy tugging the railway tie onto the train tracks. The rumble of the oncoming train became a roar.

"What the fuck are ya doin'?" shouted Otis.

"Duck!" yelled Earl. The warning was utterly useless since Otis was already lying in the ditch. He did, though, heed his own advice and threw himself flat. The train grew out of the darkness and brushed away the railway tie like a mosquito. Wood splintered into toothpicks and flew off into the night. The engineer, not knowing what he had hit, applied the brakes full force. Sparks lit the prairie sky as the sixty-four car freighter slid down the tracks. Long before it had come to a complete halt, Earl and Otis were safely ensconced under a pile of tractor parts on a flat car. Destination: Vancouver.

05

In absolute defiance of everything Vancouver, birds were singing and the sun was shining. The previous evening's rain had headed inland. A rogue crow swooped into the park to scare off the other birds. Cawing loudly, the obnoxious bird brought Meatboy back to the land of the living. The battered punk rocker tried to open his eyes but only one would function properly—the other was swollen shut. He sat up slowly and painfully. Where the hell was he? He couldn't remember a thing. His hands gently probed the many bumps and abrasions that covered his head. It felt like a football. Bits and pieces of the fractured evening began filtering back into his consciousness. The stage-diver, the PCP, and the three loogans in the pickup truck all came back like one of those revenge movies where the good guy first gets the shit kicked out of him. It never failed to amaze him that even in the nineties, you could still be assaulted simply for the way you looked. Meatboy almost never went looking for trouble—it went looking for him.

Fearing the worst, he checked his pockets. His cash was still intact. At least his attackers hadn't robbed him. Looking around he saw he was in a park, but he didn't know which one. He'd visited Vancouver twice before, but both times he had been so drunk he remembered nothing in terms of geographical significance. Right now, though, his whereabouts were of little importance to him, he didn't even know if he could walk. His entire body felt like it had been worked over with a ball-peen hammer. Giving himself a quick check for broken ribs, he discovered one of the cans of beer in his leather jacket had ruptured under the attack. Blessedly two still survived. Gratefully, he popped a tab and took a sip of warm beer. Meatboy winced as the alcohol stung his split bottom lip. Despite his many aching lumps and bruises, he decided that he would live. He'd been beaten worse than this before; the cops in Toronto had hospitalized him once just for jaywalking and a little cheek. There was never a video camera around when you needed one.

The park where Meatboy had made his last stand was your typical urban camping spot for junkies and the homeless. Several feet away, a used syringe hid in the grass like a poisonous snake. The lack of beer cans would have been conspicuous if it were not for the fact they were worth ten cents each. Surprisingly, none of the park residents were home. At least nobody had set him on fire.

The warm beer went down slowly but it made Meatboy feel a little better. The sun felt good on his bruised face, and if he had a cigarette things wouldn't be so bad. He cast an eye about the park for someone to bum a smoke from. The park was still empty but twenty feet away, leaning against a park bench, was his brand new back-pack. He certainly couldn't recall taking it to the show last night, so what was it doing here? Groaning aloud, he got to his feet and went to reclaim his property. As he got closer, he saw that it wasn't his backpack after all— this one was a lighter shade of blue than the one he had acquired just before leaving Toronto. Meatboy looked around to see if the owner was anywhere nearby. The only person in sight was a shopping cart lady who trundled slowly by. If the pack was hers, it would be on the shopping cart.

Handicapped by weak morals, Meatboy considered the options. He could limp away and let somebody else claim the lost property, or he could take it down to the police station and turn it in. Fat chance of that happening. He was allergic to cops. Maybe he should just take a little look inside to see if there was anything worth stealing. After all, finders keepers, losers weepers. Right? Bulldozing guilty feelings aside, he undid the buckles and opened the pack. Inside, a white plastic garbage bag topped up the pack. Probably somebody's dirty laundry, thought Meatboy disappointedly. Fumbling with the oversize twist-tie securing the bag, he noticed there was a fair bit of dried blood between his fingers. If only it wasn't all his. Seconds later he forgot all about his most recent thrashing. Nothing in his wildest dreams could have prepared him for what he saw next. The bag was filled to the top with stacks of tightly bundled hundred dollar bills.

The world twisted slowly on its axis as Meatboy's heart skipped a beat and went into orbit. He was tempted to pinch himself to see if he was dreaming, but he was already in enough pain. This had to be real; most of his dreams involved drinking and fucking, not money. Financial success was not high on his list of priorities, but this kind of money boggled the mind. Realising that he was just standing there, mouth hanging open, Meatboy quickly refastened the backpack and hoisted it to his shoulders. This was no time to think, he had to act. Leaving the park without looking back, he wondered exactly what the hell he was going to do with so much money. Having this kind of responsibility was almost like work. Just worrying about how to keep it safe was stressful, and walking around with a backpack crammed full of money wasn't a very good idea. He'd probably get drunk and leave it on a bus.

Before Meatboy traveled very far, he recognized a street sign. In last night's inebriated stupor, he had walked the wrong direction and ended up on Victoria Drive. He hailed a passing taxi, refusing the driver's offer to put his pack in the trunk. Giving the cabbie Paula's address, he sat back to contemplate this latest turn of events. How could anyone accidentally leave so much cash in a city park? He could only imagine himself making such a serious fuckup. Most people wouldn't trust Meatboy with anything more valuable than a toothbrush.

The taxi pulled up in front of Paula's apartment building on McLean Street. Meatboy looked in the rearview mirror and was startled by the sight of his own battered face. He looked like a nightmare on Elm Street. The cabbie was also watching him with concern, probably just for his own safety. Not wanting to alarm the driver further, Meatboy yanked some cash from his pocket and thrust a hundred dollar bill into the cabbie's hand. "Keep the change," he instructed. Tugging the backpack from the car, he slammed the rear door and waved good-bye to the shocked cabbie.

Meatboy had no way to tell what time it was, but judging from the lack of pedestrian traffic and his exhaustion, it had to be pretty early. He hoped Paula hadn't gone to work yet. It was Saturday but this detail had completely escaped him. Pressing intercom buzzer number 1287, he waited anxiously for the sound of Paula's voice. After what seemed like an eternity, a sleep-heavy voice answered.

"Hello?"

"Let me in, Paula, it's me!"

"Meatboy?"

"Yeah, let me in!"

Anger woke Paula up fast. "Why should I let you in, you jerk! Do you know what time it is? Is Silvi with you?"

"Naw. C'mon, let me in. I got something important to talk to you about!" A note of desperation crept into Meatboy's voice. There was a lengthy pause as Paula considered. Against her better judgment she buzzed him in.

An old man wearing a puke green cardigan and slippers with dress socks eyeballed Meatboy distastefully as he entered the lobby. The nouveau riche punker suddenly felt above such discriminatory observations. He pulled out a couple of crumpled twenties and stuffed them in the old duffer's sweater pocket. "Get yerself some new slippers, grandpa," he ordered. There was no point in handing out money if you couldn't at least offer a few helpful suggestions. Before the old man could react, Meatboy stepped into the elevator and the door closed behind him.

Paula was sitting on the couch wearing a ratty house-coat when he let himself into the apartment. Her jaw jutted pugnaciously, but when she saw the condition of his face, anger turned to alarm.

"Holy shit! what happened to you?"

"Aw, you know, the usual redneck bullshit. Say, you got a cigarette?"

Paula quickly fumbled for a smoke from her pack on the table and jumped up to place it between Meatboy's swollen lips.

"You look pretty rough." She lit his smoke with a Spiderman lighter and frowned concernedly.

"Yeah, yeah. I'm alright," he said taking in a lung full of smoke. "Listen, you're not gonna believe what I just found in the park!" He dropped the backpack on the floor and looked meaningfully at Paula. She stared back, uncomprehending.

"You found a backpack in the park?"

"Look in the pack!" said Meatboy excitedly. A corner of his mind wondered if there actually *was* any money in the bag, or if he had just dreamed the whole thing up. Paula crouched down and undid the buckles on the pack. She opened the bag and gazed in at its contents.

"Holy shit!" she gasped, "You found this in the park?" Pulling out one of the bundles of cash, she flipped through it with her thumb. "How much is here?"

"Beats the hell out of me," said Meatboy unaware of his poor choice of words. "I came straight here from the park, I haven't counted it or nuthin'." He went into the kitchen and got himself a beer. Fortunately the fridge door stayed on its hinges. Messy reminders of his prank still littered the floor. Paula burst in, her face flushed with excitement.

"What are you gonna do with all this money?" she squeaked.

Meatboy took a quick pull on his beer. "Why are you askin' me so many questions? I was hoping you could help me decide what to do. I've never had more than two thousand dollars at one time. I haven't a clue what to do." The adrenaline of the find was wearing off and his face was throbbing in time to his pulse. He staggered back into the living room and dropped onto the couch. Paula trailed behind waving the bundle of cash.

"But what are you gonna *do*?" she persisted. Her brain was working overtime. Along with her joy at Meatboy's good fortune, she also feared that a windfall could have dire consequences. People didn't just throw money away.

"Gimme a break!" moaned Meatboy. He was one hurting unit.

Paula tried to show her guest some sympathy, regardless of how superficial it might be. Even though wealth had never been a priority for her, it was hard to think of anything but the money.

She went to the bathroom and got a warm cloth to clean Meatboy up a little. Sitting down next to him, she dabbed gently at the dried blood that encrusted his face.

"Ow!" he complained before realizing that the warm cloth felt good and that he enjoyed the attention. "Well, the money's not doing anybody any good sittin' here. I figure we should take a bunch of it and do some partying." He was having a hard time suffering with so much cash to blow. It shouldn't be too much trouble to have some fun with that much money.

Paula did the best she could with Meatboy's face. It wasn't like he had a lot of good looks to spare, but at least he looked a little better. The idea of going on a tear with this much money kind of scared her but the temptation was just too strong to resist. She put the bloody cloth down on the table.

"It's pretty early. What do you want to do?"

"I dunno. Let's go for breakfast."

Paula shrugged. Breakfast sounded harmless enough. She picked up her leather jacket and house keys. "So let's go then."

Meatboy finished his beer and got painfully to his feet. He was going to go out and have some fun if it killed him.

"Do you think this loot will improve my chances of getting laid?" he asked hopefully.

Paula shot him a withering look. "Maybe," she said, "but not by me."

06

A loud banging awoke the stowaways from restless slumber. A railway cop was searching the cars. The Rat quickly assessed the situation and held a forefinger to his lips. Atlas was too sleepy to heed the Rat's warning, and opened his mouth to speak.

"Shh!" whispered Tommy peremptorily. "Grab your stuff and get the fuck outta here!" The sound of the prowling policeman grew closer. Cautiously, Tommy opened the door and peered out. The cop was climbing into a boxcar three doors down. "Quick! Let's go!" he urged.

"Are we in Vancouver yet?" asked Atlas picking up his guitar case. As no conductor had announced the stop, it was a reasonable question.

"I sure hope so," said the Rat. He gathered up his belongings and went to the door. The train had come to a halt deep in the belly of a heavily-overgrown ravine. Other than a highway overpass extensively covered with graffiti, there were no other indications of 'civilization'. The Rat noticed a Dunderheads logo spray-painted on the bridge.

"We're here," he told his band mates, relieved. Everybody knew the Dunderheads were from Vancouver. They climbed hastily out of the boxcar and moved rapidly down the tracks.

The C.P. cop jumped from the car he had been searching and fixed the retreating stowaways with a ferocious scowl. "Stop! Police! Put your hands in the air!" he barked fumbling with his sidearm.

"Run," the Rat said unnecessarily. The trio clomped heavily away as the cop blew his whistle and gave pursuit. Atlas lumbered into the lead while the others struggled to keep up.

"We gotta get out of this ravine!" shouted Tommy. The sides of the embankment were choked with black-berry bushes and seemed all but impenetrable. Fortunately Atlas spotted a narrow trail that wound tightly between the treacherous, spiky thorns. "This way!" he yelled plowing his way up the trail. "C'mon you guys, hurry up!"

Stopping short of the incline, the train cop looked up and saw that he would have to risk skin and clothing in order to catch the illegal riders. The hell with that. Catching train-jumpers was perfunctory, but while it was fun beating the snot out of homeless vagrants, nobody actually wanted to go to too much trouble. Besides, the one carrying the guitar case looked like he could eat policemen.

Atlas reached the top of the ravine and squeezed himself through a gap in the chain-link fence like Peter Rabbit. He set down his guitar case and spread his arms in a gesture of victory. "Yahoo!" he shouted. Shrugging off his backpack, he rolled around on the grass kicking happily. He was elated now that they had reached their destination. His companions watched him indulgently. They were used to Atlas' youthful enthusiasm, though it still seemed strange to see a grown man carrying on like a kid.

The boys looked around wondrously. The neighbor-hood they had climbed into was quiet and residential.

Modest middle class houses with well-kept lawns lined the streets. Dogs barked and sprinklers spritzed lazily. It was the kind of place they were from and hated.

The Rat looked around as if experiencing déjà vu. "Hey, wait a minute!" he exclaimed, "I know where we are. We're close to Commercial Drive in East Van! I know a girl who lives around here somewhere. Let's pay her a visit."

Atlas stopped frolicking and sat up. "We're gonna go get something to eat first, right?"

Tommy was annoyed. "Why's it always have to be about food?" Although he too was hungry, he thought finding a place to stay took precedent over his stomach. "I think we should go try to find some people we know."

The Rat nodded but knew it wouldn't be so simple. The only times Atlas deliberately disobeyed him was when food was involved. His assumption was correct.

"You promised we'd go to a restaurant and eat everything on the menu twice!" wailed Atlas, looking ready to burst into tears.

"Aw, crud," said the Rat to Tommy. "You know this guy will never shut up if we don't get him some chow." As much as a situation warranted it, the Rat never swore.

Atlas cheered visibly. He got to his feet and picked up his guitar case. Things were going his way. "Which way to the restaurant?" He smiled enthusiastically with big white teeth.

Tommy threw up his hands in defeat. "Awright, for fuck's sake let's get this over with!" he said with resignation.

The Rat pointed east. "I think it's this way."

Atlas quickly shouldered his pack and began marching in the chosen direction. He would have walked trustingly to the end of the earth in any direction the Rat pointed, confident that a Burger King would be just over the next hill. His mates tagged along behind, hungry and tired from the long trip. "Slow down a bit, ya big ape," grumbled Tommy.

The city was alive with things green and growing. Flowers and plants of every size and colour blossomed from every nook and cranny. Tommy waited expectantly for insects to bite him, yet only a fragrant breeze filled the air. This was as close to paradise as he'd ever been. "Muddafuck!" he said, slightly awestruck. "You sure we're in Canada?"

Atlas crossed the street and started looking frantically for a food vendor. "There's one over there!" he said pointing to a Portuguese restaurant on the other side of the road.

"Looks closed to me." Or at least a sadistic part of Tommy's nature wanted it to be. Atlas raced across the street nearly being struck by an early morning bus. It was hard to say who would win, and who would lose in such a collision. By the time Tommy and the Rat joined Atlas on the other side, the starving guitarist was slumped defeatedly against the side of the building.

"It's closed!" he weeped. This time, tears actually did roll down his cheeks. He was inconsolable.

The Rat knelt down beside him. "Cheer up, big guy. This is Commercial Drive, there are hundreds of restaurants here."

Atlas looked at him, eyes brimming with tears. "Yeah, but will any of them be open!" Once he made up his mind to be heartbroken, he really went for it.

Tommy had almost reached the end of his rope. "Look, ya big baby, there's another one right over there!"

He nodded to an awning half a block down that advertised "Wings Restaurant-Open Early" in big, bold letters.

Dim hope flickered behind Atlas' eyes. "Well, I suppose we could go look," he ventured.

To Atlas' delight, the establishment was open. The punks stepped blinking into the dim interior. Other than a wary Chinese waitress wiping the tables, the restaurant was empty. The hungry stowaways dumped their worldly possessions on the floor, and without waiting to be seated took a table.

"FOOD!" cried Atlas in a loud, triumphant voice. The reluctant waitress dropped three menus on the table and turned to leave.

"Wait! Don't go, I'm gonna order right now!" Atlas said anxiously. He flipped hurriedly through the menu. "I'll have two deluxe cheeseburgers with bacon, a spanish omelet, a large order of fries with gravy, a roast chicken, a clubhouse sandwich, and two chocolate milkshakes." Satisfied, he tipped back in his chair and beamed broadly at his mates. "So what're you guys having?"

Tommy gaped at the gluttonous guitar player in disgust. "You mean you're going to eat all that yourself?"

"Sure am!"

Tommy and the Rat settled for cheeseburgers and fries. The waitress brought them a pitcher of water and left to convey their wishes to the chef. Atlas loosened his belt in preparation for the feast that lay ahead.

"So who's this chick we're gonna visit?" Tommy asked the Rat. He wondered what she looked like. Girls were never far from his thoughts.

"I met her at a D.O.A. show last time I was here. Ended up at her place later. She's a fashion victim, but man you should see her legs."

Tommy wanted to know more but knew the Rat wasn't one to kiss and tell. "I hope she doesn't mind a little company," he said glancing across the table at Atlas. The salivating guitar player could hardly be described as 'a little company'. "She might put up with us if we can kick her back some money from our welfare checks. If we apply this morning, we could have a check by this afternoon."

The food began to arrive quickly, as if the restaurant owners wanted to be rid of their guests as soon as possible. Atlas seized a greasy cheeseburger and demolished half of it in a bite. Taking several chews, he paused thoughtfully and picked up the ketchup to squirt it directly into his mouth. Spillage ran from his chin. Tommy and the Rat ignored Atlas' table manners and began eating in only a slightly more civilized fashion.

Still more food arrived—barbecued chicken, spanish omelet, chips and gravy, all slid into the famished guitarist's bottomless pit. The harried waitress did her best to bring food and remove debris, but before long the table was covered with chicken bones, overlooked french-fries and puddles of gravy. Tommy and the Rat watched Atlas with disgusted awe. It was like watching a bad car wreck—horrifying, but hard to look away. At length, Atlas belched loudly and leaned back in his chair picking his teeth.

"You finished?" asked Tommy.

Atlas picked up a stray fry and popped it into his mouth. "Yup," he said chewing noisily and patting his swollen stomach. The waitress brought the bill as the cook, suspicious, stood by the cash register with arms folded menacingly on his chest.

"Sixty-three dollars and fifty-two cents!" gulped Tommy. He didn't think they had that kind of money, and the cook didn't look like a very understanding sort. He glared at the boys.

Atlas began to sing quietly:

Dine and dash at the China Kitchen,
we eat for free and the food is bitchin'.
In and out like a twenty dollar ho,
when we get the check we blow."

"Oh, shit," warned the Rat. "Whenever he starts singing that Lummox number, it means he's not gonna pay."

"Are you nuts!" Tommy hissed. "We'll never get away with this!"

"Sorry, guys," said Atlas apologetically. "I don't have enough money. We're gonna have to make a run for it." Brushing crumbs from his lap, he got up abruptly and picked up his guitar case.

"You fuckin' asshole!" wailed Tommy also getting to his feet. If they were going to run, he wanted to be in the lead.

"You pay now!" shouted the cook waving a meat cleaver. Atlas shoved the cook aside as the Rat issued another pointless command. "Run," he said.

Meatboy stumbled half a block away. His head was spinning and a bad hangover was kicking in. "I need beer!" he moaned. Paula put a steadying hand on his shoulder to keep him from falling.

"You sure you wanna continue? You look like you should be in the hospital." she asked giving in to concern. He looked pretty rough.

"Fuck that!" said Meatboy. "I'll be okay once I get some food and a couple of beers in me." Nothing was going to cheat him of his fun. Arriving on Commercial Drive, Paula looked around for a restaurant. It was still early, and most of the stores and businesses were just beginning to open. She didn't go out to eat very often, almost never at this time of the morning. But in view of how much money her benefactor had, Paula figured they should find the most expensive place possible.

"Let's grab a cab and go downtown to the Hilton," she suggested. She didn't want to be greedy but this opportunity wasn't likely to repeat itself anytime in the foreseeable future.

"That's a great idea," agreed Meatboy. "Unfortunately, I'll probably be dead before the cab gets there. I need food NOW!" He weaved melodramatically across the sidewalk.

Paula was beginning to tire. She wasn't even hungry but felt a sense of duty in helping Meatboy spend his money. Still, she wasn't willing to let him call all the shots. "So where *do* you wanna go then?" she asked exasperatedly.

Before Meatboy could answer a door in front of them flew open, and a huge punk rocker carrying a guitar case smashed into him with the force of a White Freightliner. As the sidewalk rushed up to meet him, other people came running out of the restaurant and tripped over them like a ten car pileup on the freeway. The wiry Chinese cook brandishing a meat cleaver stood over them screaming.

"You pay now!" he yelled shrilly, seizing the guitar case lying on the sidewalk.

Meatboy fought to untangle himself from the human wreckage. The brick shithouse that had crashed into him regained his feet first and stood howling on the sidewalk.

"That's my guitar!" shouted the freeloading punker. He wanted to rush the cook; only the swinging cleaver kept him at bay. His companions also stood well back but were no longer attempting to flee. Paula had managed to avoid being knocked down and watched helplessly from the sidelines. Meatboy reached out a hand to her and she hauled him to his feet. Shaking his head like a punch drunk boxer, he shouted with righteous indignation.

"Hold it! Hold it! What the fuck is going on here?"

"You pay me sixty-three dollar and fifty-two cents, or I keep guitar!" shrieked the furious cook. He turned to the waitress hovering in the background. "Phone police!"

"Hang on a bloody second!" said Meatboy pulling cash from his pocket. "No need to call the cops." He separated two hundred dollars from the thick wad of cash and handed them to the cook. "This should settle things." He wasn't used to being able to buy his way out of tight spots. It was a high he had never tried. The cash instantly mollified the cook/restaurant owner, who put the guitar down on the sidewalk and pointed at Atlas with the cleaver.

"You very lucky friend pay bill. Next time not so lucky!" With this prediction, the cook turned and stalked back into the restaurant.

Atlas gave Meatboy a sheepish look. "Tanks, man. We didn't really wanna see the police." Tommy and the Rat nodded in agreement.

Meatboy chuckled. "Nobody wants to see the cops. How the hell did you guys rack up a sixty-three dollar bill?"

Tommy jerked a thumb in Atlas' direction. "Are you kidding? This guy makes Friar Tuck look like a light snacker. This isn't the first time this has happened." He squinted at Meatboy. "You look familiar, we met before?"

Meatboy returned the gaze. "Naw, I don't think so, but then again there's lots of people I can't remember. No hard feelings." He changed the subject. "We were looking for someplace to eat ourselves, but I don't think it would a good idea to go in there after that shit you guys just pulled." He looked curiously at Tommy's faded STRETCH MARKS T-shirt, "Saaay, where you fellahs from, anyway?"

"We just got here from Winnipeg. We were on our way to go visit this girl, Silvi, I met last time I was here."

Meatboy rubbed his chin. "Silvi? A tall blonde, legs up to her neck? I know her."

Paula gave Meatboy a nasty look and held out her hand to the newcomers. "I'm Paula, and this is Meatboy," she said indicating her battered companion with a nod of her head. Tommy was the first to accept her hand.

"Hi! I'm Tommy, the big guy is Atlas, and the quiet one is the Rat. Our band in Winnipeg broke up, so we came out here to start up another one."

"Well, this is all fine and dandy but I'm still hungry and thirsty. Let's get a taxi and pick up some food and booze and go over to Silvi's," said Meatboy rubbing his stomach.

Paula whistled for a cab.

07

Whitney B. Porterhouse carefully trimmed the end of his Cuban cigar and leaned back in his tres chic leather and chrome desk chair. Chuckling quietly to himself over the latest screwing of his constituents, he held a gold-plated lighter to the stogie. As Minister of Transportation, he had a great deal of latitude when it came to closed door wheelings and dealings, and generally speaking it was John Q. Public who got it up the ass. The proposed Skytrain additions for example. Even though the trains are used by millions of people weekly, only a small handful had any say as to where the new stations would actually be built.

Being an election year the Premier, in his infinite wisdom, had decided that a huge construction project was exactly what the economy needed to pull itself out of its desperate tailspin. Four separate routes had been neatly blueprinted and offered to the public to see which expansion they felt would be most useful. The fact that these proposed routes were completely unreadable to the average citizen was irrelevant to the powers that be. Also irrelevant were the cost overrides and staggering deficit. The Premier's office pushed the project through cabinet, and actually went so far as to announce an impossible completion date.

True, most taxpayers supported an expansion of the heavily overburdened system. But the route for the multi-billion dollar train system had yet to be announced.

Previously worthless property could fetch astronomical sums if one of the new stations were to be built right on it. Unfortunately, the value of property around the stations would drop dramatically as crime and traffic increased ten-fold. Knowledge of where these stations would be built was like having a treasure map.

And Whitney's knowledge had turned out to be very profitable. The buzzing intercom interrupted Whitney's fantasies of how he would spend all the money he had made on this latest scheme.

"The Premier is on line one, sir. He says it's urgent," said the Minister's pneumatic secretary.

Annoyed, Whitney was forced back to the present. "Tell him I've gone to lunch." Come to think of it, that was a good idea.

"Very well, sir," said his secretary with only the slightest hint of disapproval evident in her voice.

Whitney sighed. Why was he always expected to work? Stubbing out his cigar in a cut glass ashtray, he rose reluctantly and plucked his hat from its elegant rack. He figured a couple of martinis should help him get through the afternoon. Nodding to his secretary, Whitney stepped out of the office into his private elevator, dropping rapidly to the ground level thirteen floors below. Electing to leave his Mercedes in the parkade, he headed out to the club on foot. It was a pleasant spring day, and being a fitness buff, he always enjoyed the exercise. Suddenly he was aware of a presence next to him.

Whitney looked over and his jaw dropped in surprise. "Leo! Where the fuck have you been? I've been expecting to hear from you all morning! So, did things go smoothly?" Mounting tension caused him to increase his pace.

Leo struggled to keep up, his gait more of a prance than a trot. "I'm afraid not sir. We've got a problem."

Whitney's black heart skipped a beat. "You better not be telling me you screwed things up," he said with alarm.

Leo paused. He hated to be the bearer of bad news. "Don't be angry with me, Whitney. I went to the park at four o'clock like you said, and I looked all over but I didn't see a backpack anywhere." He waited fearfully for his boss to explode. He could be so nasty when he was angry.

Surprisingly, Whitney remained outwardly calm although inside he was seething. He had lived up to his end of the bargain, and if Braden thought he could screw him out his money, there were going to be serious repercussions. Without turning to look at his lackey, he dismissed him gruffly. "Just go home. I'll call you later." He further increased his pace. Leo was left behind on the sidewalk; he called to Whitney.

"I'm sorry, Whitney!" Leo was heartbroken over failing him, his misery only made worse knowing Whitney didn't see how much he loved him. Dejectedly, he turned and walked slowly back to his car.

Whitney was furious, but not at Leo. He knew the simpering little fag would never have the gumption to rip him off. This had to be Braden's fault. Never trust a criminal. His smooth face twisted into a gross facsimile of a grin as he realized the poetic justice of him being swindled. He arrived at the club, and with a nod of the head to several of his bureaucratic cronies, took a table in the back of the small, dimly lit room. Ordering a double vodka martini, he tried to figure out what had gone wrong. He probably should have handled the pickup himself, but generally he tried to stay out of East Vancouver at night. Besides, that was what Leo was for. Aside from his clerical duties, he also helped Whitney with his dirty work.

Intentionally dropping some change on the floor, he got himself a good eyeful of cleavage as the waitress bent to retrieve it. Whitney batted strictly for the hetero team despite any romantic designs Leo might have on his ass. Though he would never admit it — not even to himself—it did excite him that he was attractive to both sexes. At age forty-six, Whitney was slim and possessed sleazy, GQ good looks. Other than his fondness for the occasional cigar and his penchant for vodka martinis, he took a great deal of care in his personal grooming and worked out regularly in his own gym. The ugliness within was not reflected in his outward appearance.

Killing half of his drink at a gulp, Whitney tried to hit on a course of action. There were a number of sneaky ways he could get even with Braden for not delivering the kickback but they all involved personal risk. Maybe it would be a good idea to hear what his excuse was before taking any direct action. Enemies of Braden often ended up taking dirt naps or went missing. Finishing his drink, Whitney got up to use the pay phone. Organized crime links not withstanding, he wanted his money.

According to Nash Braden's income tax return, he was in the car upholstery business. But after only the briefest of conversations, it became clear to anyone who knew anything about upholstery that even on a good day, Mr. Braden couldn't even tell the difference between naugahyde and neurotoxin. Which is not to say Nash wasn't a professional, it was just that being an extortionist, illegal gambling parlour owner, drug trafficker and all-around bad guy didn't look very good on a tax form. At this moment he was going through last night's receipts from his three illegal casinos. One of his top employees seemed to be skimming off the top. He would take a couple of the boys to go sort him out later on. It was always such a sad thing when people got greedy.

Dismissing the recalcitrant employee from his mind, Nash took a small sip of Scotch and put his feet up on the desk. Last night's payoff hadn't gone exactly as planned. He had wanted to handle things differently but the pompous politician had insisted on all this silly cloak and dagger stuff. It had been his intention to stick around to make sure things went smoothly but some kind of fight had broken out down the street. He had placed the backpack against the agreed-upon bench and scrammed. If that slimy politician had any brains at all, he would have been waiting to snatch up the pack as soon as it was dropped. Nash was uncertain of Porterhouse's skills in skullduggery, and although the information the politician possessed was invaluable he didn't trust him not to cock it up. This was Nash's first venture into land speculation, and so far, it was a bit nerve-racking. He was still following this worrisome train of thought when the phone rang, causing him to slop ten-year old scotch over the rim of his glass. Cursing, he set down the glass and picked up the phone.

"This better be good!" he growled into the receiver.

Whitney was caught off guard. He had been ready to deliver a blistering attack, but Braden's blunt phone etiquette had put him on the defensive. Attempting to recover his indignity, he replied, "It's not very good at all. I didn't get your package last night."

There was a pause as Braden put things together. "What! What kind of game are you trying to pull? I made the drop, right where you wanted. Maclean Park, Georgia and Maclean, at four o'clock in the morning."

"Georgia and Maclean? I thought Maclean Park was at Georgia and Templeton!" It was Whitney's turn to pause as he considered that he might have made a very expensive geographical error. He turned pale at the thought.

"Are you trying to tell me you went to the wrong park? You don't get out to East Van much, do you?" sniggered Braden. It wasn't his fault if Whitney had fucked up. He had fulfilled his end of the arrangement.

"We agreed on Maclean Park!" insisted Whitney. "You weren't there!"

"You were at *Templeton* Park, you blithering idiot. You don't know very much about the city for an elected politician." Braden would be enjoying this more if he had already received the crucial information. He took a sip of fine scotch and waited for a reaction.

"Oh my god!" quaked Whitney. "Someone else must have picked it up!"

"Some bag lady probably has it by now. I told you we should handle things my way," rebuked Braden. He couldn't believe what a moron the Minister was.

"What are we going to do?" asked Whitney. This was his worst nightmare come true.

"Correction. What are *you* going to do?" It wasn't enough that the arrogant politician had bungled the job, Braden wanted to rub it in too.

"You gotta help me! If I don't get that money, the deal's off!" threatened Whitney.

"WHAT?" roared Braden. "Don't try to flip this back on me. You're the one what screwed things up. Do I have to remind you what happens to people who fuck with me?" His feet swung off the desk as his blood pressure climbed like an F-16.

Whitney was silent. Panic made him speak irrationally. Be calm, he told himself. He would never have made it this far in politics if he lost it every time the shit hit the fan. Still, he had no experience in dealing with a loss of this magnitude. Since blustering hadn't enlisted Braden's help, he tried begging.

"You gotta help me! What do I do? There must be a way to get it back!"

Braden also forced himself to relax. He would play along with this clown until he had delivered the goods, but regardless of Whitney's success in recovering the money a deal was a deal. This problem called for a little diplomacy. "As long as you know who's foot the shoe is on, I might be able to help," he offered tentatively.

"Oh thank you!" Whitney gushed uncharacteristically. There was no limit to the depths he would plumb for money. He was a true prostitute. "What do we do first?"

"Listen, I'm only going to get into this at an advisory level. If I was you, I would send someone down to Maclean Park and ask around. Maybe one of those street people knows something about it."

"I can't believe this is happening!" moaned Whitney. He was beside himself with despair.

"Yeah, tough break. Call me and let me know how it turns out. Either way, you owe me," said Braden hanging up the receiver. He poured himself another two fingers of scotch and tipped contemplatively back in his chair. How could he ever have gotten involved with such a complete and utter asshole?

08

It was eleven-thirty in the morning, and already things were getting loud. Silvi had been asleep when the raucous crowd had shown up on her doorstep, but it was a pleasant surprise to see Meatboy and the Rat, especially when she saw how much food and booze they were carrying. The group had had to sit and drink beer in a neighborhood bar until the liquor store opened, and by now everybody except Atlas was catching a decent buzz. Despite his mangled face, Meatboy had managed to choke down a submarine sandwich, and was now working on a triple paralyzer. The Queers blasted from mammoth floor speakers.

I started out by sniffing glue,
killing brain cells is what I wanna do.
Pissing off my mom, acting really dumb,
when you get down to it, having lots of fun.
Next stop rehab. Next stop rehab.

Meatboy was in his element. He had a captive audience; pretty girls to flirt with, tons of punk rock to play, and enough alcohol to stagger the Russian Navy. Maybe he had died in that skirmish last night. He tossed out this idea and polished off his paralyzer. If he was dead undoubtedly opera music would be issuing from the giant speakers, and instead of vodka he would be drinking herbal tea. Nope, this was the real thing. Merrily, he shouted over the blistering wall of ass-kicking punk. "So where are you guys gonna practice? Do you have all the members you need?" It was a fair question; although trios were not uncommon, most punk units usually had at least four members. The lads from Winnipeg were all sitting next to each other on Silvi's sofa like guests on the Tonight Show, unsure of who should field the question. As usual, Tommy was silently elected.

"We don't know where we're gonna practice, we don't even have a place to stay yet!" Tommy hollered back, "And we still need a singer!"

"Hmmm, well, I hope things work out for you," said Meatboy, unheard as the music was far too loud to hear anything under a yell. Realising the futility of conversation, he got up from his armchair and went to get himself another drink. It never dawned on any of them to turn down the music. That would be sin. Paula followed him into the kitchen.

"So who are you gonna tell about that money?" she asked, getting herself a Sleeman's. Meatboy hadn't bothered with any inferior brands and the fridge was loaded to the gunwales with fine, premium beer.

Meatboy glared at her. "Nobody! An' the only reason I told you was because I thought you could keep yer mouth shut." He poured a drink from the large pitcher of premixed paralyzers.

Paula shot the fire back. "If you want this to be a big secret, you're sure going about it in a weird, fucked-up way. People are going to start wondering where all this money is coming from."

Meatboy rejected this. "What, you think these guys are gonna complain? *I* sure never ask questions when it comes to a free lunch." He couldn't see how it was going to be a problem.

"Well, don't say I didn't warn you," said Paula brushing past him on her way back to the living room. As she attempted to slide by, Meatboy caught her wrist and spun her around to face him.

"Let's just stop all this shit. I wanna fuck you, and you wanna fuck me. So why are we playing this game?" Putting his hands on her shoulders, he tried to kiss her with bruised, swollen lips. Paula gripped him by the ears and pierced his soul with her eyes.

"Listen carefully, Buttmunch. I may have screwed you once, but you're not what I'm after." She released his head, and with a final defiant flash marched back into the living room.

Meatboy miserably watched the object of his affection bounce away. "What *are* you after then?" he yelled at her departing back. He figured he was falling in love.

Back in the living room, Tommy was looking around at Silvi's spacious two-bedroom apartment. It seemed she had plenty of room for a few guests. What harm could it do to ask?

"So Silvi," he called out over the thundering roar. "Do you think you could put us up for a couple days?"

"Sure, what the hell," she yelled back. People had a habit of walking into her life and staying awhile. Hoping she wouldn't regret her decision later, she watched her new guests eat. The big one was already halfway through a bucket of fried chicken, but he seemed to be slowing down a bit.

Content that they at least had a place to sleep for the night, Tommy looked longingly at their host. He wouldn't mind humming her kazoo. Draining the last of his beer, he got to his feet. Things seemed to be looking up—Meatboy had saved their asses, and he sure wasn't shy when it came to spending money. "Anybody want another beer?" he bawled.

"Sure!" yelled Silvi and the Rat in unison. Atlas shook his head in the negative, his mouth was full of coleslaw.

"*The party starts now!*" screamed Handsome Dick Manitoba from the loudspeakers.

Walking into the kitchen, Tommy found his benefactor sitting sullenly at the table, a half-finished paralyzer in front of him. He looked like a love-stricken elk.

"What's up, man? Why so glum?" asked Tommy. He got himself a beer and pulled up a chair.

"Aw, it's nuthin'. I want Paula to ride my horse, but she won't get up in the saddle." It was an awkward metaphor but he could live with it. He picked up his glass and emptied it.

"Don't worry about it, mate. I saw the way she was looking at you. I thought you two were going out."

Meatboy brightened. "You figure she likes me?"

"Oh yeah, don't worry about it. She'll come around," said Tommy with more assurance than he felt. He changed the subject. "Silvi tells me you used to sing in a band."

"Yeah, but that was a long time ago. It didn't work out."

"Whaddya mean it didn't work out? You had some fun didn't you?" pressed Tommy. "Why don't you try out for our band?"

For some reason this possibility hadn't occurred to Meatboy, but now that Tommy had brought it up, he did need something to do. The problem was he didn't really have that much faith in his singing abilities. His other bands hadn't been very well received. Still, that wasn't really the point. The point was to get really drunk and make a lot of noise. It would be fun. Especially if they didn't have to worry about getting paid. "Hmmm, maybe I will," he ventured. The idea of hamming it up onstage took his mind away from his romantic woes. He wondered if these punkers from Winnipeg could actually play their instruments. But that didn't really matter either, since he couldn't sing. But where would they practice? He supposed they could rent a jam space and some equipment. The logistics involved were so much easier when you had money.

"Did you ask the other guys about this?" Meatboy was taking the offer seriously. He poured himself another paralyzer.

"Naw, but I'm sure they won't have any objections," said Tommy. How could they after Meatboy had pulled them from the frying pan?

"Who won't have any objections?" said the Rat arriving on the wobble. He had only caught the tail end of the conversation. Weaving over to the fridge, he snagged a couple of beers.

"I was just telling Meathead here he should try out for our band," reiterated Tommy.

"That's *Meatboy*," corrected the potential recruit.

"Oh yeah?" said the Rat. He also pulled up a chair. It was easier to talk in here where the music pounded at a more conversational level. Taking a long guzzle of ale, he assessed Meatboy critically. "I dunno, Tommy. He looks pretty lame to me."

Meatboy was taken aback by this sudden attack. "Who you calling lame? Fuckface." His adrenaline surged as he prepared to do battle.

"Did I say lame? I meant to say stupid *and* lame!" challenged the Rat with a grin.

"Grrrrr!" Meatboy growled. Partly rising, he took a wild swing at the Rat's head. He was too angry to aim his punch accurately and the blow glanced harmlessly off the Rat's skull. Instantly the kitchen table was flipped over and the two antagonists were rolling around on the floor, showering beer and broken glass.

"Hey! Goddamnit! You guys cut it out!" shouted Tommy trying to separate the combatants. Meatboy had the weight advantage, but his foe was fast and wiry. Over and over they rolled, chairs and bottles flying in all directions. Atlas rushed into the kitchen, the girls hot on his tail.

"What the fuck is going on?" screeched Silvi. The fight raged on. Meatboy had the Rat by the hair and was trying to gouge his eyes, while the Rat sunk his sharp incisors into Meatboy's thumb. They tumbled into a rack of pots and pans, which came crashing to the floor. Kitchens weren't meant for this type of warfare. Atlas seized them by the scruffs of the neck and held them apart, kicking wildly. The bewildered guitarist shook his captives roughly.

"What the hell are you guys fighting about?" he roared. He thought they were all good friends.

"I was just testing our new singer," gasped the Rat. "He passed!"

Twenty beers and a bottle of vodka later, they were all like friends on a bad TV show. Everyone was crowded onto any kitchen seating available, joking, singing, and quarreling with one another like lifelong comrades. By unspoken mutual consent, they had agreed to remain in the kitchen where they wouldn't have to shout to talk.

Even Atlas had caved to peer pressure, and sipped slowly on a beer. The debris from the brawl had been cleared away, and the only reminder of the fight was a small cut over the Rat's left eye and a pile of broken beer bottles swept hastily into a corner.

Silvi balanced giggling on Tommy's knee as Meatboy and the Rat tried to best each other with tales of chaos and mayhem.

"One time," bragged the Rat, "I was so stoned on acid, I thought it would be great to stand up on a table in the Eaton's Place food court and piss all over everybody!"

"Yeah!" laughed Tommy. "You got barred six months for that!"

Not to be outdone, Meatboy chipped in with a story of his own. "I once got thrown out of a Chinese restaurant for setting fire to a stack of menus, then pissing on them to put the fire out!" Everybody laughed and drank. By now it was two-ish. It didn't look like anybody was going to the welfare office today. In the living room a Ramones CD hammered to conclusion. The Rat got up to change the disc, instantly forfeiting his chair.

"Play something a bit newer," complained Tommy. "Go eat a bug," suggested the Rat. Although all three bandmates were committed punkers, their tastes were dissimilar. The Rat was into old punk classics like The Damned, Stiff Little Fingers and Iggy Pop. Tommy preferred hardcore punk; Wasted Youth, Circle Jerks, D.O.A. Atlas played only Canadian punk, past and present; Personality Crisis, Snatch Bandits, Kraft Dinner Revenge, and The Nostrils.

The Rat went into the living room. A minute later, The Forgotten Rebels boomed from the speakers. The Rebels were old enough to qualify as classic punk under the Rat's strict criterion. Silvi was glad she had inherited her older brother's extensive collection when he had moved to Japan; although she had never heard of most of the bands these guys were playing, the collection had earned her some respect.

Paula moved her foot away as Meatboy attempted to play footsie. Didn't that guy ever give up? "So what are we gonna do tonight?" she asked. At this rate they would all be totally shitfaced by supper time. She wanted to go out and do something. Maybe Meatboy would take them all out to eat at someplace posh but then again she didn't want him to think he could buy her with money.

"I dunno," slurred Meatboy. "We'll worry about that later. Actually I was thinking of proposing a toast." He went over and got a bottle of 151 proof rum from the fridge. "I was saving this for a special occasion, but this will do," he joked.

Silvi produced a matching set of old pewter shot glasses and Meatboy filled them ceremoniously to the top.

"To the band!" he cried lifting his glass into the air.

Following suit, the assembled crowd raised their glasses.

"What are we gonna call the band?" asked Atlas holding his shot glass as if it would bite him.

"FIRE IN THE HOLE!" bawled Meatboy tossing back the hi-test.

"That's what we'll call the band," said the Rat quietly raising his drink in salute.

09

Earl and Otis were thirsty and miserable. They slipped unobserved from the flat car and made their way slowly through the Vancouver train yard. Earl had had about enough of Otis' steady bitching and moaning. One little knife wound and you'd think it was the end of the world.

"I'm hurtin' bad, Earl. Maybe I should go to the hospital!" whined Otis even though he wouldn't go near a hospital if he was suffering from multiple gunshot wounds; all he wanted was acknowledgment of his pain.

"Keep it up, and you'll be hurtin' even worse," advised his hungry partner. He was in no mood to mollycoddle anyone.

Otis fell silent but made a show of grimacing horribly and clutching at his chest like Sanford Sr. having a fake heart attack.

Earl looked at him with antipathy. "I thought it was yer shoulder got stabbed." He knew a fraud when he saw one.

"It was, but the whole area hurts!" Otis moved his hand over towards his shoulder.

Earl rolled his eyeballs skyward. "I don't know why you need to get my sympathy. I couldn't care less if you drop dead on the spot!" For emphasis he picked up his pace, leaving Otis trailing lamely behind and crying out plaintively.

"Don't leave me behind! Look! Look what I got!" Otis reached into a inner pocket and pulled out a nearly-full mickey of lemon gin.

Earl did a double take when he saw the bottle. "Wha? Where'd you get that from? You been holding out on me!" He wasn't sure whether to be pissed off or pleased. "Say, buddy, how 'bout a little drink?" He moved to Otis' side and examined his shoulder with transparent interest. "How's the shoulder?"

Unscrewing the cap with great deliberation, Otis took a tiny sip before handing it over to Earl. They were pals again.

The N.T.R.A. was a loosely organized U.S. gang divided into two main groups—both hated each other. Earl and Otis belonged to the Northern Chapter. There were no meetings, no dues, and the members were never all in the same place at the same time. The only thing holding them together was a small tattoo on the inside of the forearm. Lately they'd been getting some bad press and were suspected of being responsible for a string of railyard murders Stateside. Earl and Otis now headed towards a local hobo encampment where they might possibly meet up with other gang members. The gin was ancient history and its warming powers were fading.

"You think Shorty is still around here?" wondered Otis. Shorty was always good for a smoke or a can of beans.

"How the hell should I know?" answered Earl gruffly. With no booze, he wasn't inclined to curry his partner's favour. The train yard gradually gave way to an abandoned industrial park. Graffiti, and gang tags covered every available surface. Huge expanses of cracked pavement twinkled with broken glass; an exquisite carpet for an urban wasteland. A heavily tagged building appeared with several scruffy characters going in and out through one of its loosely boarded windows.

"What's going on here?" asked Otis. Thanks to the gin, his shoulder no longer seemed to be troubling him.

"Looks like a punk squat to me," said Earl, his interest rising. "Maybe our friends from the train are in there. We should check it out."

"Ya mean them guys what stabbed me? I don't have my gun anymore!" worried Otis. "An' there's three of them, one's pretty big!" It wasn't the same without his gun.

Earl wasn't about to let his fear show, but Otis did have a point. "Let's see if we can find Shorty or a couple of the other boys. Then we'll see what's what."

Otis shrugged. "Okay," he agreed noncommittally. "But if they have that piece, I'm splitting."

"Fer cryin' out loud, don't be such a pansy!"

"Fuck you! I don't wanna add bullet holes to my stab wound."

Earl left it alone. "Well let's go try to find Shorty. And we gotta get something to eat and drink."

"Last time we were here he was staying under the Granville St. Bridge," said Otis pointing in the direction they had just come.

"Aw, fer fuck's sake, why didn't you say something?" Earl complained.

The tired train bandits began slowly retracing their route, eventually arriving at the Granville St. bridge. To the casual motorist passing over its modern concrete span, it looks like any other. He might notice some nice landscaping that frames the exit and entrance ramps and think nothing more of it. A closer look though, would reveal an entire village built out of scavenged sheets of plywood, strips of discarded plastic, and any other rain-repellent material. Filthy clothing, syringe wrappers, and empty rice wine bottles lie in thick profusion amidst

77

the ragtag collection of shacks and lean-to's. This was no man's land; a dark netherworld for those who had fallen through the ever-widening gaps in the social safety net. As it was mid-afternoon, most of the residents were at work dumpster-diving, collecting returnable bottles, or panning. The only people left in the encampment were either too drunk or too stoned to move.

Searching through the shanty town, all Earl and Otis received for their inquiries were unintelligible threats or suggestions to perform anatomically impossible sexual acts upon themselves.

"Aw, let's forget it, it looks like he ain't here," said Otis disappointedly. His stomach was starting to cave in.

For once his mate agreed with him. "Yeah, let's go down to the soup kitchen and see if we can grab some chow." They turned to leave. Stumbling through the heavy undergrowth Earl tripped on a root, and nearly fell to the ground.

"Fuck," he cursed. "They should get a bulldozer in here and level the whole fuckin' shebang."

"Then where would all yer pals sleep?" asked Shorty rubbing his ankle. The root had turned out to be Shorty's outstretched leg. He had been sleeping under a bush that, even under the loosest of definitions, could not be described as a domicile.

"Shorty! We were looking all over for you! How ya been? Got anything to eat?" rushed Otis breathlessly.

"Whoa! slow down, I just woke up!" How Shorty had gotten his nickname was not obvious, for he stood at least five eleven in shredded Nike runners. Maybe the nickname had been given to him by a woman. Snaggle-toothed and bristling with reddish-brown whiskers, Shorty was advancing in years and no longer spent as much time riding the rails as he did in his youth. He was an irascible, short-tempered Scotsman who devoted all of his time to the pursuit of food and booze. Returning to the shrubbery, he reappeared with a bottle of rice wine.

"You're a good man, Shorty," said Earl gratefully accepting the bottle.

"Somebody has to be. You lads don't make it easy," grumbled the Scotsman.

As they worked their way through the bottle, Otis and Earl related what had happened to them at the hands of the punk rockers. Shorty made appropriate noises at the appropriate times, but seemed more concerned with getting his fair share of the liquor.

"Hey, save me some of that!" he ordered gruffly.

Otis polished the rim of the bottle on his grimy cuff and passed the jug back to his benefactor. "Here ya go. Anyway, we passed a punk squat on the way down here and we thought maybe you could help us get a few of the boys together so we could go down and pay them a visit."

Shorty didn't look too wild about the idea. "Them punkers always mind their own bizness, I got no beef with them."

Earl worked himself into an indignant state. "Check that tattoo on your forearm, are you N.T.R.A. or not?"

It took more than a moment for Shorty to consider the question and give his reply. He didn't want to start any trouble so close to home, but to openly refuse a fellow gang member's request for assistance was just cowardice, punishable by a severe beating. "Oh alright! I might be able to dig up a couple guys, but it would help if you lads had something to grease the wheels a bit, ya know, booze, money?"

"Well, if those punks have anything we can use we'll split it up even," offered Earl. Now that the wine was kicking in he was looking forward to settling the score.

Shorty once more crawled into his decrepit little hidey-hole, this time emerging with several crude weapons; brass knuckles for him, makeshift clubs for Otis and Earl. The trio began looking through the hobo jungle for other N.T.R.A. members. None seemed to be in camp at the moment.

"I thought I saw Bad Eddie here earlier, he must have gone down to the soup kitchen," said Shorty stroking his chin thoughtfully.

"Fuck it," Earl decided. "How many of them could there be? Let's just go down there and take a look around." He was thirsty and bored.

Shorty had his doubts about the mission. Hadn't a similar miscalculation wiped out General Custer and his troops of the Seventh Cavalry? Reluctantly he followed Otis and Earl out of the camp and down the railway tracks. It was turning into a fine day, not that any of the raiders noticed. They would, however, have complained bitterly had it been raining. Earl was still limping, but otherwise seemed to have recovered from the train incident. Otis, on the other hand, was still complaining loudly about his wound.

"Slow down a bit, you guys. I think I'm gonna pass out!" He teetered to and fro like a groom at an Irish wedding. His companions ignored him and continued towards their destination at a good clip. Finally the punk habitat came into view.

"So what's the plan?" asked Shorty.

"Shhhh," warned Otis. Twenty yards away, a small, tattoo-covered teenager with spiky, orange and green hair climbed out the window of the warehouse and took a fleeting look about. The raiders ducked out of sight behind an old railway siding.

"I wonder how many of them little freaks are in there?" whispered Otis.

"Why don't we grab that skinny little puke and ask 'im?" suggested Earl with a vicious sneer.

10

Meatboy, Tommy, Paula, Silvi and the Rat were drunker than seventeen sailors. Pushing a shopping cart full of booze, they caroused down the street. Heedless of police, all six carried open beer bottles. A large boom box balanced precariously atop the shopping cart as Diesel Boy ripped from the speakers:

My pants are falling down, the room is spinning round.
My stomach is making funny sounds, I'm falling down.

"Where the fuck are we going?" drawled Meatboy. They had left Silvi's after her caretaker had threatened to phone the cops. For some reason her neighbors had objected to the early morning party.

Paula noticed Meatboy's eye was turning spectacular shades of purple and magenta. "We're gonna to see some of my buddies down at the squat," she shouted. The punker headquarters was a good place to go if you wanted to get loud. The party rolled down Woodland Drive and onto Grandview Highway. With Atlas the only one of the group not completely pissed, the shopping cart wove back and forth across the sidewalk in an unsteady manner.

Paula was giddy with booze and the intoxication of sudden wealth. Going back to her job at the travel agency no longer seemed worth the trouble. Although she wasn't even fucking Meatboy, she knew how generous he could be. It would be easy to talk him out of some money. Voices in her head screamed to be heard. *Don't get mixed up in this! If you spend his money, you're nothing but a whore!* went one. *But it would be so easy!* argued the other. *Stuff that crummy job! You could live large with that much money!* It was tempting to take the money and run but somehow it was important to remain true to her code of ethics. Paula swigged on her beer and wished desperately there was somebody she could turn to for advice. Lost in thought, she failed to notice Meatboy lurch up to throw an arm around her shoulder.

"I'm gonna sing in a punk rock band!" he crowed boozily, "an' you can come and dance. We'll throw stuff around and make a lotta noise, it's gonna be great!" Tilting his head back at a 90° angle, he poured beer straight down his throat.

Paula envied Meatboy's simplicity. The guy had just found a backpack full of money, and all he could think about was starting a punk band. She wished she could forget about the find so easily, but problems and possibilities kept popping into her head. Why did money have to make everything so complicated?

"What if you suck?"

"Who cares? The more people hate us, the more shit we'll throw at 'em!"

"Yeah!" said Tommy, who had overheard the conversation, "'cept we won't suck, we'll kick ass!" His bottle of beer slipped from his grasp and crashed to the sidewalk. "Oops," he said.

"Lots more where that came from!" assured Meatboy. Normally such an accident would be a major disaster, now it was of little consequence.

Tommy plucked another beer from the shopping cart. "Thanks, man. Lissen. I don't know when we can pay ya back. I hope you kin afford all this." He was curious about the extent of Meatboy's wealth but he wasn't going to be so rude as to come right out and ask directly.

"Don't worry 'bout it," said Meatboy. "I jus' got my income tax refund." This was a bald-faced lie—as the most he had ever received for an income tax refund was two hundred and thirty one dollars and this year he hadn't even filed. Regardless, the explanation seemed to quell Tommy's curiosity.

"Well as long as you don't mind. Do you have any idea where we kin practice?"

"No," replied Meatboy unconcernedly, "but we can start looking tomorrow. Hopefully we can find some place in East Van that's not too expensive." He was so pleased that Paula hadn't shrugged off his arm that even the thrill of starting a new band was taking a back seat. He had it bad.

"Look out!" roared Atlas from behind. Meatboy and Paula staggered out of the way as Atlas and Silvi flew by. Silvi perched on top of the shopping cart with the boom box bouncing wildly on her lap, cans and bottles rattling noisily.

"Ahhhhhhhh!" she shouted. Thrills came cheap with a shopping cart and a six-pack.

"Careful with that beer!" commanded Meatboy.

On they stumbled, across a bridge, down a series of side streets and eventually they came to the edge of a railway abutment. Now the shopping cart had to be ditched since its wheels would not roll on the unpaved terrain.

"What now?" asked Tommy. There was a lot of beer to carry. Before anyone was forced to make a serious decision, Atlas hoisted the beer from the cart, staggering. "Which way do we go?" he asked unmindful of the heavy burden.

"This way!" directed Paula picking up the bag with the hard stuff. She began climbing up a small hillock, the others tramping after her. Reaching the crest, the group paused to catch their breath. Dilapidated factories and warehouses stretched below them like a scene from *Cannery Row*.

"So where is this place," gasped Meatboy. He was winded from all the activity and hoped their destination wasn't much further.

"It's that building with the big red and white skull covering its side," said Paula pointing at a run-down warehouse some hundred yards away. Below them to the right a punk tore out from behind a railway siding, three railroad tramps in hot pursuit.

"Uh-oh," said Meatboy sobering at the sight. "What the fuck is going on?"

"Hey!" said Atlas. "Those are the guys who were hassling us on the train!"

As they watched, the punker tripped on a rusted automobile fender and fell to the ground. Instantly the tramps were on him. "Fuck off!" screamed the punk, "Get the fuck offa me!" His attackers began stomping ribcage with brutal enthusiasm.

"That's one of my friends!" shouted Paula. She ran down the hill towards the scene of the assault, intent on helping her comrade.

"I don't like those guys!" Atlas announced to the world before setting the beer down and lumbering after Paula.

"We better go help out," sighed Meatboy.

"Don't worry," said Tommy. "Those dudes haven't got a chance against Atlas." Casually, they ambled down the hill to offer their services. By the time they got to the bottom, Paula had jumped into the fray.

"Leave him alone, you assholes!" she yelled, attempting to drag her besieged friend to safety. Otis looked over at the feisty female who had crashed their little party.

Where the hell did she come from? Then he noticed the horde of punkers descending the hill towards them. This was exactly what he had been afraid of.

"Shit! Look out Earl, we got company!" he warned as a female fist crashed into the side of his head. "Fuck! That hurts!" he cried out in pain and shock. The terrified punker, who seconds earlier had been the victim, now saw his opportunity to turn the tables. He jumped up and planted a Doc Marten into the closest tramp's gonads.

"Ummpphh!" grunted Shorty. He stepped backwards clutching his balls.

All was bedlam as combat began in earnest. Atlas stepped into the melee. Swinging a colossal fist at Otis' head, he miscalculated and almost fell to the ground as his punch went wild. Realising that the blow would have knocked his head off, Otis returned the attack out of fear. His punch bounced off Atlas' chest with no discernible effect. Seconds later he was knocked flat by a shot from one of the other punkers. Birdies tweeted and chirped in his head. Earl fought desperately, bringing his club down on Atlas' thick skull. Outnumbered, the battle quickly turned against the tramps.

"Let's get the fuck outta here!" yelled Otis. He had no stomach for being shit-kicked. Earl was unable to answer, he was engaged in a losing struggle with Meatboy and Tommy. Shorty, meanwhile, was fighting with The Rat and was attempting to avoid having his nose chewed off. In the distance, a car kicked up dust as it sped towards them.

"Fuck!" said Shorty breaking free. "It's the cops!" He turned and began hobbling away as fast as his injured testicles would allow. The fighting punks also noticed the arriving police car.

"Time to scram!" shouted Tommy. "Let's go!" All the combatants scattered and ran as the police car grew nearer, with punks heading up the street and bums fleeing into the depths of the train yard. Silvi waited by the stack of beer, street-side.

"Hurry up, you guys!" she yelled.

Atlas reached Silvi first and began loading his arms with beer; there was no time to spare. Gasping and panting, the rest of the group arrived. Tommy looked back to see one of the cops running up the hill towards them.

"STOP! POLICE!" shouted the cop.

"Run," the Rat said calmly.

Dodging traffic, the fugitives darted across the busy street and down a back lane. After a half block of flat out running, they slowed their pace. It was unlikely the train cops would make a serious effort to catch them. Meatboy was exhausted and his battered face was throbbing.

"Think it would be okay to go back to your place, Silvi?" he asked.

Silvi was also feeling worse for wear. She hoped her caretaker had calmed down a little. He was an ornery old prick.

"Yeah, but you guys gotta keep it down a bit."

"What happened to your pal?" Atlas asked Paula. The punk they had rescued was nowhere to be seen.

"He probably ran back to the squat," hoped Paula. In the confusion, she had forgotten all about her scrawny friend.

"What the hell was that all about?" wondered Meatboy. "You know those creeps?"

"Yeah, those fuckers tried to rob us on the train," answered the Rat. "We kicked their asses that time too."

"I don't like those guys!" Atlas was certain on this point.

"I hope those punks at the squat don't get hassled because of this," voiced Silvi. A girl she had gone to school with lived there.

"Well, there's nothing we can do about it now," said Meatboy philosophically. The incident had had a sobering effect on him and he cracked open a fresh beer in an effort to undo this tragic happenstance. Suddenly he remembered the backpack full of money at Paula's place. A tremor of anxiety ran down his back and danced over his liver. Money meant trouble. Maybe he should just take the bag back to the park and let it be a burden on someone else. Even as he thought this, he knew he would never do it. He could party for months with this money. What the hell was he thinking?

"What happened to the rum and whisky?" he inquired.

A guilty look marred Silvi's angelic face. "It rolled down the hill when you guys were fighting."

Meatboy shrugged and kept walking. His mind was already back on the subject of money. He knew he should go over to Paula's and do something with it, but what? Clearly it was too much to worry about. As if on cue, his legs buckled and he collapsed rubber-like to the concrete.

Paula rushed over and knelt by his side. Struggling to remember her first aid, she checked his vital signs. His pulse was okay, and he seemed to be breathing alright, in fact, he was snoring.

"What's wrong with him?" asked Tommy worriedly.

"Probably just drunk and tired," said Paula getting to her feet. Tommy looked over at Atlas. Atlas knew what to do. He set the beer down, picked Meatboy up like a sack of potatoes and looked questioningly at Paula.

"I guess we're going back to my place," she sighed. Maybe she should charge him rent.

11

Leo parked his Ford Tempo half a block away from Mclean Park and checked his reflection in the rearview mirror. Satisfied his thin, straw-coloured hair was neatly combed, he got out of the car to assess his surroundings. People around here took one look at his button-down cardigan vest and neatly pressed trousers, instantly pegging him for an uppity, downtown geek. The Eastside made him nervous.

Today, however, nobody paid him much attention. On a park bench, two Natives sat quietly sharing a bottle of fine, twist-cap wine. A shirtless bum lay spread-eagled on the grass, drunkenly soaking up the late afternoon sun. All was tranquil.

The mission Whitney had sent Leo on was completely beyond what he was capable of. Whitney might as well have asked him to win the money back hustling pool. He had already concluded the only thing he could accomplish today would be getting his ass kicked. What was he supposed to say? "Excuse me, Mr. Junkie, sir. Have you seen a million dollars lying around here somewhere?" It was hopeless. Leo picked a park bench as far away from everyone else as he could and sat bitterly contemplating the situation. As he tried to work up the courage to begin questioning the park's patrons, the shirtless man sat up and scratched his greasy head with dirt-imbedded fingers. Leo panicked; the man was staring directly at him. Getting to his feet, the bum shambled over to Leo and stretched out a filthy hand.

"Say, buddy, ya got a quarter?"

Leo nervously fumbled for some change. All he had were three one-dollar coins and a few pennies. He extended a dollar and tried to figure out how he would word his questions.

"Do you know anyone who might have found a blue backpack here early this morning?" The simplest way was best.

The bum looked at him like he had radishes growing out of his ears. "Why? What's it to ya?" Generally the only people who asked him questions were policemen, and he wasn't fond of those guys.

This attitude was exactly what Leo had been afraid of. Still he pressed on. He handed the bum another Loonie. "I was just wondering if anyone's been buying a lot of drinks today."

The bum treated Leo to a contemptful, unblinking stare. "Just you, sucker," he chuckled. Jingling the coins in his hand, he shuffled out of the park and disappeared whistling down a side street.

Exhaling slowly, Leo realised how wound up he was. He was damp with sweat and his sphincter muscles were clenched up tight. Again he asked himself how he had gotten mixed up in this mess. He knew the answer, however. He was doing this for Whitney. He had been the personal assistant to the Minister of Transportation for nearly three years, and from the very start Whitney had involved him in a series of low level scams. But this latest act of corruption really had him spooked. If the stakes were this high, wouldn't it stand to reason that the chance of being exposed would be even greater? The whole thing was an exercise in dangerous futility. He subconsciously accepted the fact that Whitney would never return his affection, and that he should distance himself from this pathetic situation as soon as possible. But unfortunately for Leo, he couldn't get past his mad infatuation with the charismatic politician. He still had a job to do. With the realization that honey attracts bees, he left the park and drove to a bank machine.

The liquor store was doing brisk business when Leo arrived. The sun was shining and, as usual, people were thirsty. Purchasing four bottles of sherry and a mickey of vodka, he drove back to the park wondering if he would be beaten or arrested for his efforts. As he parked, he noticed that several other people had shown up. A fat white guy and his toothpick-limbed girlfriend sat at a picnic table rolling a joint. By the water fountain a bag lady with a heavily laden shopping cart was sitting on the grass massaging her feet through industrial-strength stockings. The Saturday afternoon party crowd was as comfortable in the park as flies on a donut.

Bracing himself, Leo carried his purchases over to a vacant picnic table, and opened one of the bottles of sherry. Now he had their attention.

The Natives got there first.

"Hey parch, how about a little drink?" asked the less taciturn of the two.

"We got our own cups," offered his companion.

"Sure, pull up a chair!" said Leo in what he hoped was an inviting, friendly tone. His new companions quickly filled their glasses with the toxic grape. Then the fat guy and his girlfriend ambled over to Leo's table and sat themselves down. Taking a large haul on his marijuana cigarette, Fatso addressed Leo.

"So what's the deal? The food bank deliverin' wine nowadays?" He had a natural suspicion of free handouts.

"I'm not from the food bank, but you're more than welcome to have a glass of sherry," Leo offered eagerly.

The paranoid pot smoker squinted at Leo. Picking up the bottle apprehensively, he tilted his neck and drank directly from the jug. The Natives glared at him; they didn't want his germs all over the bottle. The fat guy eyeballed Leo suspiciously.

"So what's the catch?" He passed the jug to his girl-friend but didn't offer to share his reefer.

"No catch. I just wanted to get to know the people around here, see if maybe anyone has noticed any strange occurrences lately."

The skinny chick sized Leo up with wary, streetwise eyes.

"The only 'strange occurrence' around here is some west side geek buying drinks for a bunch of total strangers." She took a large hit from the bottle and wiped her mouth with bony fingers.

This seemed to be the general consensus. One of the Natives retrieved the bottle of sherry and topped up his and his companion's glass. "What kind of strange things?" he asked trying to give the stranger with something for his wine.

Leo wasn't quite sure. "Well, anyone acting differently, or spending lots of money. Or maybe just the absence of somebody who is usually present?"

"You talk funny," observed the skinny chick opening the second bottle of sherry. "We ain't seen nuthin' strange, 'cept you," she added.

"Let me think," said the more talkative of the two Natives. "There's always something strange going on around here." It was beneficial to him to be as cooperative as possible.

"There was some gangbangers hanging out just before you got here, but that ain't new or strange," said the fat guy trying to figure out exactly what Leo was looking for. He reached for the bottle.

Leo considered. They didn't seem to have seen anything, and if gangbangers had found the pack it was history. The wine was disappearing fast. With the second bottle gone, Leo still had nothing. Against his better judgment he accepted the bottle from fatso, carefully wiped the mouth, and took a small sip. Maybe they would open up a bit more if they saw him drinking too. Shuddering, he swallowed the grape-flavoured gasoline. He looked around at his guests. He would have to be more specific.

"Were any of you here early this morning?"

The assembled group exchanged glances. They were afraid the booze supply would dry up if they gave the wrong answer. All were silent.

"I was here early this morning," came a voice from behind them. All heads swiveled around. It was the bag lady. Apparently she had been eavesdropping on the conversation. Slowly she made her way to the table. Leaning over Leo, she stage-whispered in his ear, "I seen lots of strange goings-ons early this morning, very strange things indeed!"

Leo recoiled from the woman's fetid breath. "What did you see?" He didn't want to get his hopes up; the old lady might start telling him about an alien invasion she had witnessed. The bag lady rubbed her fingers together in the universal gesture for money.

"I don't drink," she hinted.

Once again, Leo dug for change. He might as well gamble another dollar. Pushing the coin into the bag lady's fingerless glove, he pressed for details.

"What did you see?"

"I might have seen a young man here early this morning, he was badly beaten up." She eyed her golden goose craftily.

So far this scant information was of little use to Leo, but he had a feeling there was more. At least she wasn't talking about aliens or trying to save his soul. "What else?" he asked eagerly.

"It's gonna cost you more than a buck," said the bag lady shrewdly. Her breath was reminiscent of a seafood dumpster at high noon.

Leo was in too deep to turn back now. In an effort to conceal the contents of his wallet, he slipped it from his pocket and held it below the tabletop as he checked his funds. He hadn't been prepared for a large outlay of cash, and Whitney hadn't given him any spending money. All he had left was thirty dollars, and none of these people would take credit cards. He took out a ten spot and slipped it to the bag lady.

"What did you see?" he repeated.

The informant glanced at the others sitting at the picnic table. They were working on the third bottle of sherry and listening intently to the conversation. Things were getting interesting.

"Let's talk over there," she suggested, nodding towards the other side of the small park.

"Aw, c'mon, let us hear. We won't say nuthin'," whined the fat guy.

Leo shrugged apologetically and got up to follow the bag lady over to a small hill crowned with an abundant maple tree.

"I saw a fella here this morning," she rasped. "Had blood all over his face and was drinking a beer."

"What else?"

"After a while he got up and went over to that park bench there and looked in his backpack." She pointed with a stubby finger.

"What colour was the backpack," Leo asked excitedly.

"I couldn't really tell, it was still kinda dark."

"Blue! Was it blue?"

"I don't know, could have been."

"What did he look like?" Leo's adrenaline was over-loading.

The crafty look returned to the bag lady's crinkled eyes. "It'll cost you," she said making the rubbing motion with her fingers. She sensed she possessed valuable information. Leo quickly forked over his last twenty bucks.

"What did he look like!"

The bag lady tucked the cash into the dark recesses of her bulky winter jacket. "Funny looking. He had green hair and lots of earrings and chains. Oh yeah, he had an upside-down Canadian flag on the back of his black leather jacket. Ha, ha."

"Green hair? Was he a punk rocker?"

"I guess that's what you call them. He looked the same as all those other freaks who loiter about on Commercial Drive washing car windows and panhandling."

"What else?" Leo pumped.

"Nothing. The guy picked up his pack and left."

"Which way did he go?"

The bag lady pointed a half-gloved finger in the direction of Commercial Drive. "He staggered off thataway."

Leo sensed that he could not gain much more from this conversation. "Thank you very much for your time," he said politely. He glanced back at the picnic table. The occupants seemed to have gotten over their initial dislike of each other and were working amiably on the vodka. They were too busy drinking to notice Leo wave good-bye.

Leo was so excited he called Whitney at the number he had been told to use only in emergencies. The Minister abruptly answered.

"I hope you've got good news," he said without pre-amble.

"I did learn something." Leo didn't want to get Whitney's hopes up by being overly optimistic, but he did want to please him.

"Well, for god's sake, what is it?" Whitney demanded.

"Apparently a punk rocker found your backpack."

"That's good news?" said the Minister with agitated disbelief.

"He shouldn't be that hard to find, he has green hair and has recently been beaten."

"Oh great!" moaned Whitney. "Green hair in that neighborhood. That should narrow things down a bit!" he said sarcastically. Still, he was quietly pleased Leo had learned anything at all. Actually, things could be worse—a punk rocker might leave town or start spending money like King Faruk on vacation. The thought turned Whitney's legs to jelly. This had to be resolved quickly.

"Listen up, Leo," he said. "You're gonna dress up in your rattiest clothes, go down to Commercial Drive, and you're not coming back until you find my money!"

There was silence at the other end of the line as Leo digested the new orders. "When do I start?" he asked submissively.

"Now," said Whitney hanging up the phone. He had been wondering if the tricky crook had dropped the money in the park at all. Looking out the window of his palatial home, he realised Braden wasn't trying to rip him off. Now all he had to do was find a rich punk rocker. How hard could that be?

12

Meatboy stumbled into Paula's bathroom, and aiming with a blind eye, took a five minute piss. Finally he finished his business and zipped up. With a sense of dread, he risked a peek in the mirror. Yep, it was him alright. And he still looked like he had walked into a wood chipper. At least he was a rich, ugly motherfucker. Maybe he should just buy himself a new face.

Paula's bedroom door was closed. Being rejected every night sucked farts out of dead buffaloes. After being shot down in flames he had stretched out fully dressed on her couch. It was no fun falling asleep with a broken heart and a dick hard as a diamond cutter. If there was any justice in the world he would be skiing Paula's wonderful slopes at this very moment.

Meatboy shook his head to erase the pornographic Etch-a-Sketch on his brain. He wished there was another cure for hangovers besides more beer. Unfortunately he couldn't let fatigue slow him down, he had things to do. He quietly removed five bundles of cash from the pack beside the couch and stashed them in a hallway closet behind a stack of sweaters. Moving quietly, he picked up the backpack and stepped into the hallway, shutting the door gently behind him. It was time to put the money someplace safe.

Outside everybody was staring at him as usual, but around here it was probably his smashed-up face rather than his clothing or hair that drew the attention. Why did people have to gawk every time you got a black eye?

Ignoring the impudent turds, Meatboy walked down to Commercial Drive and hailed himself a taxi. He was starting to get the shakes from so many consecutive days of drinking. Getting drunk everyday was a tough job, and he'd been working overtime. Hell, he should be president of the company by now. He decided not to drink today and focus on finding a spot to practice. Just making the decision made him feel a little better.

Arriving at his destination, Meatboy gave the cabbie a hundred dollar bill and told him to keep the change without even suggesting how to spend it. He was still too wasted to be witty.

The bus station was full of the usual riff-raff. Three haggard prostitutes scratched posterior regions while a group of gangbangers hung out by the vending machines practicing their bored/cool look. If it wouldn't put them all out of business, they would install a crack vending machine. A kiddie pimp and two of his young boys dodged Meatboy as he made his way towards the bank of lockers. Despite the many unsavory characters that inevitably haunted bus terminals, the lockers were still a relatively safe place to stow things hot or illegal. There were too many cops around to actually take a crowbar to them. For twenty-five cents, Meatboy squeezed the backpack into a locker and pocketed the key. Politely refusing two offers to buy cocaine or heroin, he left the bus station and stepped out into the crisp morning air. He felt better now that the cash was secure. He transferred the key from his pocket to his left, stainless steel nipple ring — if he lost the key, he would know about it. He got into another cab and gave the driver Silvi's address.

Meatboy watched excitedly from his perch halfway down the hill. The Sixth Annual Soap Box Derby was about to begin. Ten shiny racers lined up at the top of the hill. Mothers, fathers, friends and family formed a tight knot on three sides of the contestants. The starter held his pistol in the air. BANG!

In car 32, little Tommy hunched over the wheel of the bright green racer and zoomed into the lead. He and Meatboy had worked on the car all summer and it was in top form. Two cars edged away from the rest of the pack. Tommy still in the lead, but with car number 11 coming up fast. Mentally urging the car to go faster, he looked over to see if he was winning.

The ten-year old driver in the next car could see he wouldn't be able to overtake Tommy in time. The finish line was coming up fast. As a consolation prize, he stuck out his tongue and screwed up his face at the competition.

Tommy grinned triumphantly. The race was his! Then, without warning, both front wheels of his racer wobbled wildly and flew off, the undercarriage sending up a shower of sparks as metal scraped concrete. The tiny racer spun hopelessly out of control and careened into the path of car 7, operated by Gerry Bristol. Highly lacquered wood splintered and shopping cart wheels zipped through the air as the two cars collided in a breathtaking smash-up. Both cars slid brokenly to the bottom of the hill as car 11 took the checkered flag.

"Haw! Haw! Haw!" screeched little Meatboy. It was the funniest thing he had ever seen. He laughed so hard he lost his foothold and tumbled down the hill, landing in a tangled heap of arms and legs. An infuriated Tommy pulled himself from the wreckage and stood over him, dripping blood from his cuts and scrapes.

"You did this!" he pointed an accusing finger. Meatboy couldn't answer, he was laughing so hard tears rolled down his cheeks in an uninterrupted flow. Tommy jumped on Meatboy and began flailing at him with tiny, impotent fists.

"I'll never forgive you for this! Never!"
"I'm sorry," laughed Meatboy, "I just couldn't help it!"

"Six dollars and sixty-five cents," the cab driver gulped worriedly. His fare had scared him considerably with his battered countenance and vacant expression. He waited to see if his passenger had the ability or inclination to pay. Meatboy thrust a hundred dollar bill at the driver through a slot in the window and slithered out of the cab. After the incident with the racer, Tommy had treated him with hostility and anger. He was relieved Tommy didn't remember their childhood association. Besides, it seemed unlikely his former pal would still foster ideas of revenge, and there was no dividend to be had from reminding him of the prank.

Meatboy sensed it was still early but he hoped the band would be awake by now. Stumbling into Silvi's lobby, he studied the intercom and struggled to remember which apartment she was in. He pressed what he hoped was the right button and waited for a response.

"Hullo?"

Meatboy recognized the sleepy baritone. It was Atlas.

"Hey, man, it's me. Let me in."

"Meatboy?"

"No, it's the fucking Son of Sam. Let me in!"

"Cool. Ya gonna shoot somebody?"

Meatboy couldn't tell if his bandmate was joking or not but the buzzer sounded and he was admitted. He was totally floogled but really wanted to find a place to practice. It was too bad they had to go to so much trouble to rehearse. He just wanted to get out there and blast out some tunes. So much money and so little time.

Atlas was eating Cheerios out of a large salad bowl when Meatboy let himself into the apartment.

"S'up, mang," said the hulking guitarist with a mouth full of cereal.

"Me, barely," Meatboy answered. "I thought we could see about getting a place today. Where's everybody?" He looked around the apartment. Other than the Rat, curled up sleeping soundly on the carpet, it was empty.

Atlas nodded towards the closed bedroom door. "Tommy and Silvi are in there," he said taking in another massive mouthful of cereal.

A knowing smile cracked Meatboy's healing lips. "Well, at least somebody's getting laid. Let's wake those lovebirds up and get this job done."

"Where's Paula?" asked Atlas. Although Meatboy and Paula were not officially an item, Atlas considered this a technicality and figured it was only a matter of time before nature took its course.

The question started Meatboy's motor. He had briefly forgotten all about the object of his desire. "Hmmm, I better give her a call."

Meatboy shook hands with his new landlord and dropped the keys into his vest pocket. "Phew! That was a hassle!" he said as soon as the landlord had departed. "I thought we'd never find a decent spot." They had spent the entire day rejecting one place after another for various reasons. Some of the joints they had seen were clearly not meant for human habitation but were well populated with rats and cockroaches. The boys didn't mind a few bugs but they didn't want too many non-paying guests. With just one more place to check on their list, they were surprised to discover that the warehouse was perfect for them, right down to the stack of pallets they intended to build a stage from. It had been no easy task finding a centrally located place yet had no neighbors within complaining range. It was a little larger than they had originally planned but the more they thought about it, the more it seemed ideal for their needs. They could have a few parties complete with bands, a cover charge and beer sales. They might even make a little money.

"Sheeeit! This is great!" stated Tommy. He didn't think Meatboy had enough money to rent a space this big. It occurred to him that the source of his wealth was well beyond the scope of any income tax refund but Tommy wasn't about to kick a gift horse in the head.

"Yeah, it ain't bad," admitted Meatboy. It was more than he'd hoped for.

Even Paula was impressed. "I guess you won't need to stay at my place anymore."

For a moment Meatboy looked disappointed, then his happiness returned. "We'll have to get a few couches of our own."

"Hey you guys!" came a shout from above them. "Check this out!" Atlas' head poked out a loft window at the rear of the hall. "There's a cool little room up here!" A loud thump sounded and then Alas reappeared rubbing his head. "But it has a pretty low ceiling."

"That could be the Rat's room," suggested Tommy. The drummer was the shortest of the group.

"You guy's aren't supposed to live here you know, this is zoned for commercial use only," Silvi reminded them.

"What the landlord doesn't know won't hurt him," said Meatboy. "Tomorrow we can go out and get some equipment but tonight we should have a little celebration." He had already forgotten about his decision not to drink. Looking about at the hundred and fifty by fifty foot warehouse, he could already imagine the place crammed full of people drinking beer and bopping to his band. At the rear of the warehouse, a roll-up garage door was big enough to accommodate a van or truck. Next to it was a heavy steel door. The hall was perfect.

"How far is the beer store?" asked the Rat. They had thought about an earlier warehouse merely for its close proximity to a liquor store.

"The Waldorf Hotel is just over on Hastings," said Paula, "We can walk there."

"Let's go," prompted Meatboy.

On the way back from the beer store they noticed two beaten up couches lying out by a dumpster, and with little effort, the couches were carried back to the new digs and arranged in a corner. An empty wire spool made a coffee table. Atlas hauled out his electric guitar and began strumming. Without an amplifier it wasn't loud, but to Meatboy's delight the guitarist could really play. Atlas knew a wide array of punk rock standards and classics. Out came the Ramones, early Clash, The Dead Boys and the Damned. But he was just playing them to build Meatboy's confidence in his ability. As soon as he had everybody's attention, he started playing songs no one recognized. One particularly catchy tune caught Meatboy's ear.

"What's that one called?" he asked.

"That's an old Stretch Marks song called Electric," Atlas informed them. Meatboy cursed himself for not recognizing it; he prided himself on his knowledge of obscure punk trivia. Atlas abruptly changed songs and began playing a ragged cowpunk style. Meatboy listened excitedly.

"What's that?" he asked hoping it was an original.

"I dunno, I'm just fuckin' around," shrugged Atlas.

"Great!" said Meatboy pulling a scrap of paper from his pocket. "Maybe these lyrics will fit. Take it from the top!"

Atlas started from the beginning, Meatboy began to sing:

Well, I was born on a farm in a hurricane
A bolt of lightning through my brain
My whole body leaking like a sieve
Mama said son, yer too stupid to live.
awright!
giddown!
yeehaw!

He repeated the first verse several times because that's all he had. After awhile Atlas stopped playing.

"What do you call that?" he asked.

"Cowpoke Blues," said Meatboy proudly, "You like it?"

"Sounds good to me," said Tommy. "I like that badder-than-Hank kinda shit. It sounds like yer chewin' on barbed wire and spittin' out two-penny nails."

The Rat nodded in agreement. "I wish we had some gear," he lamented.

"Aw, don't worry about that," Paula said. "I have a feeling that little problem will soon be solved." She looked over at Meatboy who was flush with excitement. Maybe he wasn't such a bad guy after all.

"Yeah!" Meatboy declared. "Tomorrow we're gonna go to Long and McQuade and go shopping!"

The other band members looked at each other, afraid to speak the unspoken. Finally the Rat broke the silence.

"Uh, listen we've been meaning to talk to you about all this money you've been spending. Are you rich or something? Do we have to pay you back for all this?" He waved his arms indicating the warehouse, the beer, everything.

Meatboy was quiet for a moment. "Well you might say I'm not exactly broke, and no, you don't have to pay me back. I want this band to happen just as bad as you guys. I know we haven't even jammed yet, but I think this thing is gonna work out fine." Finishing his speech, he polished off a beer and pulled another from the case beside him.

More silence. There was nothing anyone could say.

Atlas cracked open a beer and hoisted it high. "FIRE IN THE HOLE!" he shouted.

The group clinked bottles and drank deeply.

"Let's order some pizzas," suggested Atlas.

13

Nash Braden watched the beating with grim satisfaction. The errant blackjack dealer begged for mercy.

"Please, I'll never do it again!" Blood flowed from the cuts on his face and head. Two of Braden's henchmen held the victim's arms while a third worked him over with a leather-covered lead sap.

Braden took a step back to make sure no blood splattered on his conservatively cut grey flannel suit. "Oh, I'm certain of that Larry." He nodded to his employees. One goon held the victim's hands while another bent his fingers backwards. The bones snapped with a sickening crunch. The now ex-dealer screamed in agony.

Leaning over the wretched employee, Braden pulled a silenced .32 caliber automatic and stuck it into his mouth.

"No, no augghh!" screamed the victim.

"Say good-bye creep." Nash pulled the trigger. The hammer clicked on an empty chamber. Yanking the gun from his ex-employee's mouth, teeth breaking, Nash wiped the barrel off on the sobbing dealer's shirt and kicked him violently in the chest. He fell to his knees then slumped to the ground, gasping for air.

"Get out of town. Today. If I ever see you again there'll be a live round in the chamber," Braden decreed. The mobster and his goons dusted themselves off and got into a waiting limousine.

The stretch Cadillac moved slowly down the dirt road and back onto Kent. Braden focused his attention on a much larger problem. This Skytrain deal was beginning to upset his delicate digestive system. Normally he would never make such a large payoff without receiving the goods, but Whitney had promised him that he would deliver the information well before any final routes were made public. It wasn't like the politician had anywhere to run, but maybe it was time to light a little fire. Pulling a phone from his jacket, he punched in Whitney's home phone number. It was Sunday, hopefully the slippery jackass would be home.

Whitney picked up the phone on the second ring.

"Hello?"

"So, did you find your money yet?" Braden never wasted time on pleasantries.

Whitney took a moment to get his conversational bearings. "Oh, it's you. No, not yet, but I'm working on it. A million bucks doesn't just disappear."

Yes it does, thought Braden. "Well, good luck," he said without meaning it. "When do I get my package."

Another pause, "I should have it by tomorrow afternoon. I'll call you to set up a meeting."

"Tomorrow afternoon then. Don't let me down, Whitney." Braden switched off his phone and put it away. Why did he feel the politician was stalling him? His stomach rumbled threateningly.

Whitney looked at the dead telephone in his hand and cursed. It looked like he was going to have to hand over the information even though he still hadn't received any money. He wished he could blame this all on Leo. Maybe he should call the little faggot. Punching Leo's number into the keypad, he gazed contemplatively at the bottle of vodka behind the wet bar. Leo answered on the first ring.

"Hi, Whitney! I was hoping you'd call."

"Why? And how'd you know it was me?"

"I wanted to hear your voice, nobody else has this number."

"Don't talk like that! You know I hate that shit! Nobody else has your phone number?" Whitney was disgusted and amazed.

"No. When my phone rings I know it's you."

"Yecch! So where are you?" Whitney knew that Leo's love kept him enslaved but he certainly didn't want to hear about it. Unfortunately, communication with him was essential.

"I'm at the Waldorf Hotel on Hastings. It's the closest hotel to Commercial Drive. In the morning I'll do some shopping and try to talk to some of the punks."

Whitney didn't have any better ideas; the plan sounded as good as any, and he was anxious to get off the phone. "Okay, call me as soon as you have any important news."

"You know I will, Whitney. I'll do my best to find your money."

Whitney quickly hung up the phone before Leo could say anything else embarrassing. Jesus, this situation was getting worse all the time. He reached for the vodka.

It was Leo's turn to look at a dead telephone. Sighing, he set down the receiver and asked himself again why he was doing this. Why couldn't he say 'no' to Whitney? Maybe if he got the money back Whitney would be happy enough to be honest with himself and realize his true love had been in front of him all along. Stretching out on the lumpy hotel bed, he dreamed of the day when they would be together.

Outside on the street, a beer bottle smashed.

"Ya know, those punk rockers are really starting to piss me off," said Earl rubbing a large bump under his eye. Otis nodded in agreement. His head felt like an alligator had been chewing on it. He'd had enough.

"Let's just forget about those guys, even their bitches hit hard." Being whupped twice in a row had taken the jib from his jab, and now the festering wound on his shoulder ached like seven kinds of hell. He was willing to pretend he had never met any punk rockers.

Otis and Earl had managed to escape the clutches of the train police, but Shorty—unable to run quickly enough with impacted testicles—had been nabbed and taken off to jail for outstanding warrants. Unwilling to let any of Shorty's food or drink go to waste, Otis and Earl had moved into his camp and helped themselves to all available victuals. Three cans of BBQ beans, a half dozen food bank bagels, and a large chunk of moldy cheese had already been hungrily devoured. Otis searched through Shorty's humble abode in an effort to find anything else that might have been overlooked. Underneath a rancid pile of clothing he made a joyous discovery. Two bottles of Mountain Man Thunder Wine winked up at the happy tramp.

"Check this out, Earl!" he cried. "That fuckin' Shorty was holding out on us!" He lifted up a bottle for his partner's inspection.

"Good for him," said Earl reaching for the bottle with a grubby paw. "I would have held out on us too."

The wine mellowed ill-tempers and eased their aches and pains, but inevitably bitter feelings returned.

"We can't let those freaks get away with this," said Earl working on the last of his wine. "We owe it to ourselves to find them fuckers and stomp 'em into the ground."

"You and whose army?" asked Otis. "They got a whole warehouse full of backup, and what do we got?" He was hoping he could talk his partner out of any future acts of pain and humiliation but suspected this wouldn't be easy. If there was one thing Earl was good at it was holding grudges.

"We'll find some help. Those punks ain't gonna get away with this." Grumbling, Earl polished off his wine.

The sun fell out of the sky like a rotten orange, and with darkness came the cold. The tramps shivered silently for a time until Otis noticed a fiery glow in the distance. "Hey look! Somebody has a fire!" he said, getting to his feet, "Let's go warm ourselves up."

Earl wanted to argue just because it was his nature, but it was hard to ignore the fact that he was freezing his ass off. Cursing Otis, the frigid night, and humanity in general, he tossed his empty bottle into the bushes and hauled himself upright. They stumbled blindly through the darkness, getting lost twice before finally locating the source of the fire. In a small clearing, four shabbily-dressed men stood warming themselves over a fire they had built in a fifty-five gallon barrel. Startled by the sound of the approaching tramps, the men turned belligerently towards the uninvited guests. Snarling and vicious, these tramps looked like they could gargle with gasoline and shoot flames from their assholes.

"What the hell do you guys want?" growled a large, brutish-looking young man. He looked like an escapee from a chain gang.

"Uh, we just wanted to warm up a bit," said Otis. He looked hopefully around the fire for a familiar face but all he found were hostile glares.

Earl decided to take a chance. "Anyone here N.T.R.A.? We just got into town from the U.S."

The campers exchanged suspicious glances. After much muttering and more nasty glances, the young man spoke up. "There might, or there might not be, 'pends who's asking."

"I'm Earl, and this here's Otis." Both men rolled up their sleeves to reveal their N.T.R.A. tattoos. A silence descended on the camp. The brute stepped forward.

"I'm Bad Eddie," he said with no trace of irony. "These boys are all N.T.R.A. You're welcome to share our fire." He held out a hand which Earl eagerly accepted.

"So how long are you guys in town for?" asked Bad Eddie.

"Just long enough to collect a welfare check, then we're gonna roll on down to Los Angeles for the winter. It rains too much here."

"I just got back from L.A.," said one of the other N.T.R.A. members. "You gotta have a car to survive down there, and the cops will chase you all the way to Mexico for a parking ticket."

"I know a broad down there has a car," said Earl.

Bad Eddie clapped Earl on the back. "Hooeee! Yer goin' all the way to L.A. just to get yerself a little poontang? Ha-Ha-Haw! Here have a snort!" He produced a bottle of Seagrams No. 7 and passed it to Earl.

"I never been to L.A. Been almost everywhere else though," said Otis.

"Better git yerself a gun," said the bum from L.A. "Everybody down there has one. I'm Tornado Jones, and those tramps are Stovepipe and Bumticker." The gang members all shook hands.

"I had a gun," said Otis, "but I lost it on the train."

"He didn't lose it," offered Earl. "We got in a tangle with some punk rockers and he got stabbed."

"You guys let some punkers take your gun away?" Bad Eddie asked incredulously. He snatched his bottle from Otis.

"Well, one of them punk rockers was seven feet tall and biggern' you," Otis said defensively. "Fuckin' guy looked like Frankenstein, bolts and all." He was exaggerating, but not by much.

"Where'd all this happen?" asked Tornado Jones. The flickering fire revealed a cowlick that stood up on the back of his head like a miniature cyclone.

"The first scrap happened on the train, then we got into another fight with 'em when we got into town," Earl explained.

"Is dat how ya got da shiner?" asked Bumticker. His piercing blue eyes peered at Otis and Earl down a long, pointy nose.

"Yeah, we went to check out their squat and they bushwhacked us," Otis complained.

"You mean that building down the tracks with that big skull on it?"

"That's the one," said Earl.

"Why don't you firebomb the place," suggested Bad Eddie. He took a hit from his bottle and passed it around.

"Cause I wanna kick the shit outta those turkeys personally," said Earl. Just thinking about the punkers drove bamboo shards under his fingernails. "I'm gonna get a welfare check on Monday, and I'll get you all drunk if you help me fuck those guys up."

Bad Eddie slapped Earl on the back again, nearly knocking him into the fire barrel. "We'll be glad to help you out. Won't we, boys?"

14

Fire in the Hole were like hyenas in the hen house. They bounced around strumming and banging on instruments with glee and abandon, a harried salesman following them anxiously around the store. By now he had learned that even the scummiest-looking people were capable of dropping enormous bundles of cash.

"That's a particularly fine instrument, I recommend it highly," said the salesman about the Fender bass guitar Tommy was pounding on.

"What?" shouted Tommy. He had the volume cranked to eleven.

Meatboy stood watching as plate glass windows shook and customers cringed in the background. "We'll take it!" he yelled to the salesman, an impressed grin glued to his battered face. Tommy could really smack that thing. The salesman began punching numbers into a pocket calculator. He liked these guys better all the time.

In a different section the Rat was laying down a rock steady beat on a simple, but enormous Tama drum kit. Meatboy came over and bopped his head in time to the rhythm.

"An excellent choice!" screamed the salesman. This was too good to be true.

"Do you like this kit?" Meatboy hollered at the Rat. The drummer smashed out his approval with a drum roll and a cymbal crash.

"We'll take those too!" yelled Meatboy. The store was louder than a train wreck at an oil refinery. More numbers on the calculator. The salesman could already see the La-Z-Boy he intended to buy with his profits. Then it was time to look at public address systems. Meatboy plugged a microphone into a twelve channel, 1500 watt Peavey amplifier.

"Is this loud enough?" he asked the band. His voice boomed out of twin JBL studio monitors and shook tiles in the ceiling. The band nodded their heads in the affirmative. By now, most of customers had fled the store to quieter places, like bomb testing facilities or the rifle range. The salesman didn't care, he was wearing earplugs and his fingers were getting gloriously sore from entering numbers into the calculator. Paula walked into the store, wincing at the barrage of disjointed music— none of the musicians were playing the same song. She came over to Meatboy and tapped him on the shoulder. Startled, he spun around, nearly dropping his microphone. He hadn't seen Paula coming.

"Did you get the van?" he yelled over the caterwauling.

Paula nodded. "Yeah, it's parked out front!" Renting a van had been simple enough even though she had to put down a huge deposit. Meatboy was thinking about buying a van, but for now, getting the musical gear was top priority.

"Are you guys almost ready?" she shouted. The boys had already been in the store for an hour and a half. She felt left out; nobody had asked her to be in the band. She wished Meatboy had been elected only for his money but she admitted to herself that the group fit together like warts on a witch. But it bothered her that he had moved the loot without saying anything. He had a lot of nerve, trying to fuck her when he wouldn't even trust her. Money complicated everything.

Meatboy already felt like a rock star. "Let's get this done!" he shouted to the salesman, pulling packets of cash from his black leather jacket. The clerk's eyes lit up like Nagasaki at midnight.

"Yes, sir!"

But the transaction wouldn't be that simple. They still had to pick up guitar cords, strings, sticks, and all the other implements of destruction. By the time they were ready to go the girls were fast asleep in the back of the van. Paula roused herself sleepily as the boys emerged from the store lugging their new purchases. With much arranging and rearranging, they were just barely able to squeeze themselves into the van. Meatboy clambered into the front seat.

"Time to wake up the neighbors!" he said enthusiastically.

Back at the new digs, the Québécois punkers Meatboy had hired to build the stage were screwing the last sheet of plywood into place. The punks had insisted on being paid in beer. René, the lead carpenter, eyed the new gear with curiosity and opened a can of beer.

"What did you do? Rob a bank, eh?" Bank robbery was a favorite Montreal pastime.

Meatboy pretended not to hear and tried to help the band set up the equipment, but not knowing what he was doing, he just got in the way. Eventually he gave up and joined the beer-guzzling frenchmen.

Paula was tired and hungry. "We're going home," she told Meatboy. "We'll take the van back, I'll give you the deposit money tomorrow."

"Aw, don't go!" pleaded Meatboy, "In a few minutes we're gonna kick some ass!" As he spoke a guitar amplifier came to life behind him. KERRANG! Everybody's favorite, the E chord. TUM! TUM! TUM! pounded the bass guitar. TATATATAT! snapped the snare drum. A charge of electricity jolted through Meatboy's nervous system, butterflies fluttered wildly in his stomach. The band was waiting for him.

"I gotta go!" shouted Paula over the sound check. "Silvi's already in the van!" She turned to walk away.

"Wait! Don't go!" begged Meatboy. He wanted to show off. Paula, though, was too tired for any male posturing and she left out the back door without looking back. Frustrated and horny, Meatboy stomped over and jumped onto the stage. The nervousness disappeared as testosterone took over. The band started playing a song he didn't recognize. It sounded like Indy 500 meets the Ramones. Without even thinking about what he was going to sing, he screamed into the microphone.

I know a girl, man, she's so hot.
We drink, and we drink, and we talk, a lot.
but every time I try to get near,
she spits in my face and rips off my ears.
She's squeezing out sparks and I'm pickin' em up.
She makes me feel like a mucky pup.
She's the swinging queen of the underground.
But when I get close, she just puts me down.

Why, oh why, oh why won't she fuck me.
Why, oh why, oh why won't she fuck me.
Why, oh why, oh why won't she fuck me.
She's making me scream, why won't she fuck me?

Atlas smiled fiendishly and blistered into a short, angry solo as Tommy hammered the bass like a mortal enemy. Behind it all, the Rat threw down a beat as solid as pressure-treated concrete. Stunned by the ferocious attack, the carpenters jumped up and began slamming violently. Even though they barely understood English, they knew what punk rock was about. The song smashed to an abrupt finish. Feedback screamed from Atlas' amplifier as the band paused to collect itself. None of the members had expected things to click this quickly.

"Who the fuck are you guys?" asked René.

"Fire in da Hole," Meatboy told them importantly. He turned to Atlas, "What do you call that?"

"Our other singer had a different name for it, but I like your version better."

"I hope I can remember the lyrics."

"No worries. If you forget, we'll just have Paula walk by," joked Tommy.

Meatboy's frustration threatened to return but the high of creative energy filtered out the pain. "Let's try it again," he said reaching for a beer.

15

Whitney B. Porterhouse ate a bowl of high-fibre cereal and carefully brushed his teeth. Setting the burglar alarm, he picked up his car keys and stepped into the garage. He didn't know it yet but he was about to have a hell bitch of a day.

Things started out innocently enough. His secretary brought him his espresso and he sat back to browse the *Wall Street Journal*. Try as he might, he was having trouble concentrating on his morning ritual. As a person who had devoted his entire life to the pursuit of monetary gain, the matter of the missing funds weighed heavily on his mind. A portion of his brain accepted the fact that the money, or at least a large portion of it, might never be recovered. Quitting wasn't his style however, and there was no way he was going to spare any of Leo's effort to retrieve it. Visions of firm, ripe breasts danced in his head as he reached across the desk and buzzed his secretary.

"Anything important on the agenda today, Angela?" His thoughts went from gazoonkas to golf. This might be a good day to hit the links and get his mind off this mess.

"As a matter of fact the Premier just called, he wants you in a closed conference at eleven o'clock." She didn't mind being the rain on his parade.

"The Premier? What the hell does he want?" Such hastily called meetings were not part of the usual protocol. He frowned as he tried to figure out what could possibly be so important.

"I really don't know, sir. You'll have to ask him." She knew the question was rhetorical, but felt obliged to answer anyway. Angela hoped they were planning a tar and feather party for the pompous, self-serving S.O.B. For Christmas he had given her a card with the inscription, CONGRATULATIONS ON YOUR PROMOTION TO MY SECRETARY. As if sharpening his pencils was the crowning achievement of her career. Merry Christmas, indeed.

"Oh, alright," said Whitney as if there was an alternative. "Hold all my calls so I can get ready."

Whitney switched off the intercom and leaned back in his chair scowling. All he needed now were more complications. Trying to guess what the topic of the meeting might be, he went back to his newspaper and noticed that his stock in Apple had dropped three and a half points. If this trend continued he might as well just go home. Fighting the urge to nip at the pint of vodka in his desk drawer, he glanced at his Rolex. It was already ten-thirty. The meeting was in half an hour. Checking to make sure his information to Braden was in order, he unlocked a bottom drawer and removed a thin paper folder. The exact route of the Skytrain route was clearly indicated on the documents. Two particular locations along the proposed corridor were currently vacant, but were soon to be highly valuable pieces of property. Armed with this information, Braden would become a very wealthy man. Now if he could just find his own money.

The intercom buzzed.

"Time for your eleven o'clock appointment, sir."

Startled, Whitney looked again at his wristwatch. It was already five of the hour. Just enough time to get to the second floor conference room. Carrying an empty briefcase, Whitney slid down the elevator to his fate.

Someone coughed as Whitney entered the conference room. The place was silent as a morgue. The Premier, his adviser, two city planners, the Metro commissioner and the city's chief engineer were already in attendance. Much sipping of water and shuffling of papers were done as the Whitney took a chair and waited anxiously.

Finally the Premier looked up from his papers and spoke. "Good to see you, Whitney. Sorry to disturb you on such short notice, but we have an item that needs your immediate attention." The Premier, a short balding man with none of the photogenic qualities a man of his position might be expected to possess, looked to the city planner to explain.

With a pleghmy rattle, the planner cleared his throat. "We have been forced to suspend the final decision of the proposed Skytrain route until we can find an alternative that is more suitable for residents of the Grandview area." Reptilian blood pumped through the planner's heart. "They've been creating quite a fuss with their damn grassroots groups. They claim our expansion will damage the environment," he scoffed shaking his graying head. "In short, it's back to the drawing board." This concise statement was something the assembled politicians were completely incapable of, which was exactly why he had been chosen to explain the situation to Whitney.

Whitney swallowed hard. "But those plans were finalized! The decisions have already been made!" This was very bad news indeed.

The Premier beat his gums for the next five minutes repeating what the city planner had already said. The delay was really no skin off his ass, as long as the bulldozers were rolling before the citizens got to the voting booths. The voting public were mushrooms—best kept in the dark and fed bullshit.

"Which route will we go with then?" asked Whitney, his brain exploding.

"We're not quite sure yet," said the chief engineer scratching his chin. "We need more time to evaluate the situation."

"How much time?"

The Premier answered in a fashion that befitted him well. "Well, if things go smoothly, with no unforseeable problems, we should have an answer in the near future."

This did not bode well with Whitney. He knew from years of experience that any statement starting with the word 'well' was apt to be complete and utter bullshit. Desperately, he looked around for signs of enlightenment. Poker faces ruled supreme.

The Premier's voice brought Whitney back to reality. "Here are the results of our latest survey. Take these, and let us know which one you think will be most suitable to the constituents." He passed a thick sheath of papers down the table to the stunned Minister of Transportation. More jaw flapping and unwarranted speechmaking followed before the meeting was finally adjourned. As usual, the politicians seemed to have been holding a contest to see who could talk the longest without actually saying anything. Reeling from the devastating news, Whitney escaped the building for the sanctuary of the club. He couldn't imagine trying to explain the situation to Braden. It looked like a four martini lunch.

Leo began his morning with a steel spring sticking into his back. Aching, he got up slowly. It was his belief that for sixty bucks a night you should be able to get something a little more comfortable than this hastily-renovated roach hotel. Searching through the clothing he had brought, he tried to select something appropriate for the mission he was about to embark on. Fortunately, he had brought along the old blue jeans he had put off throwing out. They had a slight tear in the knee. Shirts were another matter. He favoured subtle shades, and the shirt he had brought with him was anything but subtle. Swallowing revulsion, he steeled himself to don the garment. He would have given the T-shirt to charity long ago if it were not for the fact that it had been a present from his sister. On the front, it had the slogan BEER IS BETTER silk-screened on it. God knows why his sister had chosen this shirt for him. It had never been worn.

With ten dollars worth of change from the desk clerk, he stepped out onto Hastings Street. It was still early but already two crack dealers were dispensing their wares. Leo acknowledged that the dealers worked long hours with high risk and no health coverage. It was too bad that they couldn't get jobs with the government. A bunch of dope dealers could probably do a better job of running the city than the idiots currently in charge. The neighbourhood started to change as soon as he got onto Commercial Drive. Rich in colour and smell, the street was different from every other in the city, as people of every ethnic and educational background congregated freely. From Hastings heading south, the first ten blocks were mostly filled with granolaheads and lesbians. Hardly anyone looked twice at the sight of two girls necking, and nobody ever complained about the pervasive smell of ganja in the air. However Leo wasn't here to interview lesbians or potheads. Eyes peeled for enlightenment, he walked down the street in a blur of futility. A needle in a haystack would be much easier to find than a million dollars.

At the lights a squad of squeegee punks darted in and out of traffic, industriously washing windows and cadging pocket change. Punkers had stolen the traditional rights of the disenfranchised; the almighty dollar belonged to those who ran fastest. Now that Leo thought about it, all these street people worked much too hard to be candidates for city hall. He spotted a mohawked youth wearing a JESUS WAS A CUNT t-shirt energetically scrubbing the windows of a station wagon full of tourists. When they got back to Lethbrige they would have something to talk about.

Leo waited until the punk got back to his corner.

"S'cuse me, can I ask you a few questions?"

The kid squinted suspiciously, "Why, you a cop?" People down here had a natural aversion to policemen.

"No, I'm looking for someone, maybe you've seen him around."

The punk stuck out his hand. Leo put a dollar in it.

"What does he look like?"

"Green hair, a black eye, and has a black leather jacket with an upside down Canadian flag on the back."

The light turned red, traffic stopped. "Nope, haven't seen him," said the punk over his shoulder as he rushed back to his job.

Leo kept walking. Smells of all description wafted past his nose, freshly baked bread, coffee, marijuana, spaghetti sauce, stale piss from a darkened doorwell, car fumes, and anise. Grocers proudly displayed varieties of cheap produce and street vendors laid their wares out on the sidewalk. People of all description milled about shopping and dining. Punks, artists, musicians, yuppies, hippies, gays, blue collar workers of every race, and the occasional Hell's Angel bustled about their daily business. The street was a veritable beehive of activity. Leo came upon a man with a tattooed head trying to sell home-made books. A sign proclaimed him a 'Thirsty East Van writer'.

"Have you seen a green-haired guy with a black eye around here?" Leo asked. On the cover of the books, an evil-looking punk held a large revolver.

The writer pretended to think. "Nope, seen lots of people, but none of that particular description. Ya wanna buy a book?"

Leo tossed him a coin and kept moving. Someone must have seen something. He was already discouraged. Stopping for a coffee at the Continental Coffee Shop, he looked over at a group of quietly chatting punks.

"Good morning! Can I buy you all a coffee?" he asked in a much friendlier tone than he felt.

The punks reacted indifferently. "Sure, if you want," said a girl. She had so many facial piercings she glinted in the sun like the front end of an old Cadillac. The waiter took their order and went inside.

"You a reporter or sumpin'?" asked a lumpy young man with red hair and a Dunderheads T-shirt.

"No, I'm looking for my brother, I thought maybe you'd seen him." He had decided that to get results he would have to bend the truth.

"What does he look like?" asked the girl.

"He's got green hair, a black eye, and an upside down Canadian flag on the back of his jacket." Leo was smoothing out his patter.

Silence fell as the waiter brought the coffee. "I don't think I've seen anyone who matches that description," said the lumpy guy. "Could be anybody."

One of the punks turned his back to reveal an upside down Canadian flag, but it was sewn to a denim vest and the owner had short bleached blond hair. Leo's already deflated hopes sank even further. He hadn't been expecting instant results, but he had been hoping to find some trace of the elusive punker.

"Well, thanks for your trouble, have a nice day." He had a token sip of his coffee before leaving. It was fine coffee, but it could have been mop water for all the consideration Leo was able to spare. He walked all the way down to the Broadway Express Pub on Eleventh Ave. questioning people along the way and using up nearly all his change in the process. Nothing. Not a nibble. Defeated, he hailed a taxi. He was tired and needed a break.

"Where to, mac?" asked the driver.

"Waldorf Hotel," said Leo leaning back exhausted.

The driver clicked on the meter and dove into traffic. "Whatsamatter bub, you look a little down."

"I've been walking around all day looking for my brother, and I can't find a trace of him."

"What does he look like? Maybe I can help."

Leo gave him the description without hope.

The cabbie thought a moment. "A beaten up face and a black eye?"

Leo's heart beat wildly. "Yeah, have you seen him?"

"Yeah, I gave him and his buddies a lift up to Long and McQuade on Saturday."

"Isn't that a music store?"

"Sure is. Seemed like he had lots of money. Gave me an eighty-nine dollar tip. Told me to get a hair cut."

"Where did you pick him up?"

"Hmm, let me think. That would have to be on Commercial at Grant, right by the liquor store."

"Can you take me there?"

"Sure buddy, it's on the way."

Leo got out of the cab at Grant, tipping the driver generously. His spirits took a nosedive as he realised he had passed this liquor store earlier with no results. Again he went through the ritual of questioning all the weird looking people, but nobody had seen anything. Where the hell could such an identifiable person have disappeared to? He had to be around here somewhere. Whitney wasn't going to like this one bit.

16

Holding a hand over one eye to prevent double vision, Meatboy stepped on the gas and struggled to stay on the road. His newly purchased '64 Parisienne Custom Sport ragtop leapt forward. Unfortunately the four barrel V8 had more guts than the inebriated punk could handle. Skidding around a corner, the car crossed the center line and veered into the path of an oncoming semi-trailer. The truck's horn blared nightmarishly as Meatboy white-knuckled the car back into his own lane. With a rush of air the semi flew by, missing them by inches. The drone of the horn receded into the distance as the occupants of the car considered their fate.

"Stop the fucking car, asshole!" screamed Paula. Until now she had tried to ignore Meatboy's atrocious driving but enough was enough. She still wanted to live.

Ashen-faced, Meatboy pulled over onto the service lane and brought the car to a halt. The rest of the band sat silently—there were no words to express how glad they were to still be alive. Tommy released his death grip on Atlas's forearm. A more fragile person would have screamed in pain but the huge guitar player didn't make a peep. There was nothing like a brush with death to sober you up a little. Paula jumped out of the front seat and ran around the car, yanking the driver's door open. Plucking the keys from the ignition, she grabbed Meatboy by the lapels of his black leather jacket and dragged him out onto the highway.

"You fucking jerk! If I wanna die, I'll do it myself! Now get in the car and shut the fuck up!" she shrieked.

Throwing the keys into Atlas' lap, Paula issued another command. "Atlas, you drive!"

"But I don't have a license!" protested the guitarist.

"Who cares! Neither does he!" She pointed to Meatboy who had climbed sheepishly into the passenger seat, doing as he was told. None of the other band members were in any condition to argue. They had been drinking and practicing non-stop since Sunday; it was now Wednesday. Atlas, still the only one sober in the car, moved from the back seat and took the wheel. Putting the car into gear, he moved into traffic at a more sedate pace. Paula sat in the back seat and fumed.

"Id's okay now, Paula," said Tommy. "Iz gonna be alright." The near disaster was already fading from the bassist's booze-soaked brain.

Paula's rage began to subside. She was glad she had her own place to go to, for she almost certainly would have gone insane if she had to hang out with them all the time. Sobering up fast now, the guilt of missing the last three days of work was sinking in. She had tried to get to work, but somehow Meatboy had managed to talk her out of it. This was all his fault.

"Sorry, Paula," apologized Meatboy from the front seat. He had already forgotten what he was supposed to be sorry about, but he knew Paula was angry with him.

"Hey!" said the Rat, who was on the verge of passing out. "Where we goin'?"

It was a good question. What had started out as a beer and food run had turned into a pointless cruise around the city. Incredibly, they had driven past several police cars without being pulled over. Paula figured Meatboy was luckier than a boatload of leprechauns. Now they were somewhere in Burnaby, miles from home.

"Take me home," demanded Paula. If she made it to work tomorrow she might still have a job.

"Aw, c'mon over to my crib," whined Meatboy. He still hadn't gotten laid but stubbornly refused to give up.

"Fuck it, I wanna go home!" Paula insisted. This party had to end.

Meatboy suddenly gave up and got angry. "Fine," he snapped. "Atlas, take the young lady home."

"Hey! I ain't the fuckin' chauffeur! Which way do I go?" He didn't know where he was going or how to get there. Unused to the power of the modified 283 mill, he zoomed over a median and narrowly avoided side-swiping a mailbox.

"Look where yer goin!" ordered the semi-conscious Rat, fighting to keep his eyes open.

Meatboy was bitter. All this money and it couldn't even get him a bit of gash. Maybe he was going about this all wrong—if he couldn't have Paula, he was sure as hell going to get someone else. Tersely, he directed Atlas to Paula's apartment building by the shortest possible route. The car screeched to a halt. Paula got out.

"See ya later, Paula. Hit it Atlas," commanded Meatboy. He was on a mission.

"Bye, bye Paula," said Tommy. The Rat had succumbed to fatigue and he began to snore.

"Quit ordering me around," Atlas told Meatboy as he pulled away from the building. "Now where we goin?"

"Four Seasons Hotel," said Meatboy. "Now we are gonna do some livin'!"

Atlas looked out at the bright city lights from the seventeenth floor window. "Wow! This is fuckin' cool! Is this where all the rock stars stay when they're in town?"

"That's what they tell me," answered Meatboy. He gazed drunkenly into the heart of the city. Instead of feeling on top of the world he was pissed off and angry. What good was all this money doing him? Storming away from the window he tore around the luxurious suite looking for a phone. The Rat was sprawled out on the floor sawing logs. Tommy, who had adjusted to being rich in a microsecond, was having a vodka gimlet and watching porno on a large screen TV.

"Where's the fuckin' telephone?" growled Meatboy.

Tommy pointed to a cordless phone on the black glass coffee table without taking his eyes from the screen. Meatboy snatched up the phone and dialed 411. "Hello, information? Yeah, gimme the number to Madam X's Escorts on Richards St."

Tommy's head snapped over to Meatboy. Was he doing what he thought he was doing?

Meatboy disconnected and punched in the number. "Yeah, Madam X? I need some girls over here." He held his hand over the receiver and shouted to Tommy. "What kind do you want? Blonde, redhead, or brunette?"

Tommy took too long to respond. It was such a tough question. Meatboy got back on the line. "Send us one of each. I'm payin' cash. Yeah, that's right. Suite 1709, Four Seasons Hotel, and hurry!" He switched off the phone and smiled at Tommy. "Hope you boys are horny, the girls are on the way!"

Tommy nodded towards the slumbering drummer on the floor. "What about him?"

"If he wakes up, he can have leftovers." Meatboy got back on the blower and dialed room service. "Send up a bottle each of Johnny Black, Jim Beam, Cockspur rum, and two bottles of Absolut vodka. We also want five T-bone steaks with all the trimmings, some tomato juice, a carton of cigarettes, six burritos, a bottle of Maalox, and three bottles of decent champagne." He hung up the phone without waiting to see if room service had got the order right.

Atlas wandered back into the living room. "Did I hear you ordering food?" He had completely missed the part about the hookers. "I'm hungry!"

"Good thing," grinned Meatboy. It was exhilarating to spend so much money with a couple of fast phone calls. He hoped he had brought enough cash. He'd been visiting the backpack daily and already it had a noticeable dent in it.

Tommy could resist no longer. "Listen, Meatboy. I don't really give a fuck where you got all the money, but what I wanna know is if the cops are gonna nail yer ass." It was great helping the singer spend his money, but not if he had to die in some stupid shoot out for it. Tax refund? He didn't think so.

Meatboy was tired of keeping his enormous secret anyway. "You guys would never believe me if I told you."

"Try us," said Tommy.

Even Atlas seemed interested in the answer, although he was probably more concerned about when the food would arrive. Both band members looked expectantly to Meatboy.

"I found the money in a park."

Silence. Then Tommy finally spoke. You don't really expect us to believe that, do you?"

"See? I said you wouldn't believe me. I'm tellin' you the truth!"

Atlas believed him. "Wow, that's pretty lucky. All I ever found was a twenty dollar bill in a flower pot."

Tommy looked like he still had his doubts, but was not prepared to push the issue any further.

There was a knock at the door. Atlas loped over and threw it open. Instead of the food he'd been expecting, three glitzy women stood filling the doorway with cheap perfume. Atlas looked bewildered.

"You called?" asked the blonde, slightly taken aback by the size and appearance of the massive guitarist.

"Yeah!" said Meatboy from behind him. "C'mon in, girls."

The hookers hesitantly entered the suite, taking in the luxurious accommodations and the punk rockers in at a glance.

Meatboy held out a hand to the blonde. "Hey, I'm Meatboy, this big guy is Atlas, and that's Tommy."

The blonde took his hand. "I'm Sapphire, the red-head is Heidi, and the brunette is Amanda. Pretty nice suite. You guys in a band?" she figured they must be one of those new punk groups she'd heard on the radio.

"Yup, we sure are!" said Atlas. "Are you friends of Meatboy's?"

Amanda snickered, "We are if he's paying."

Comprehension flickered slowly across Atlas' face. "Oh," he said.

Two serving carts loaded with booze and food arrived. With a flourish, Meatboy signed the tab and tipped the waiter extravagantly. He was so busy grandstanding that he forgot to offer any suggestions on how to spend it.

The waiter took everything in stride—he was used to dealing with rich, grubby-looking young men. "Thank you, sir. Have a pleasant evening," he said getting a good eyeful of Amanda's abundant cleavage.

"Would you ladies care for some champagne?" offered Meatboy, peeling foil from a bottle.

"Oh, I suppose a little drink wouldn't hurt," said Sapphire. She could spot the signs of newly acquired wealth, and knew with a little encouragement it wouldn't be hard to separate cash from owner.

Tommy and Heidi disappeared into one of the bedrooms before Meatboy could even pour the champagne.

"So, what's the name of your band?" asked Sapphire sipping a glass of bubbly.

"Fire in the Hole," said Meatboy proudly.

"I've heard of you guys," lied Sapphire. "Don't you have a song on the radio?"

"We're going into the recording studio tomorrow," announced Meatboy taking a guzzle of champagne. "We're gonna be big."

Atlas looked curiously at the singer. "You didn't say nothing about that!"

Meatboy shot him a dirty look. "You weren't listening, I told you about this yesterday!"

Sapphire changed the subject. "So you boys ready to party?" she cupped her hands under her breasts and lifted them like an offering to the gods.

Meatboy jumped to his feet. "I sure am!"

"Well, let's go then," said Sapphire holding out her hand. She was the prettiest of the three, so she naturally assumed Meatboy would pick her.

"Uh, no offense, but if it's okay with you, I'd rather go with Amanda."

Sapphire tried not to let the rejection show. "Sure, makes no difference to me."

Amanda looked surprised; she usually got picked last. Her dark hair was cut in a short, choppy style and she wore little makeup. She allowed Meatboy to lead her into one of the three bedrooms.

Meatboy kicked the door closed and quickly stripped off his clothes. He playfully tossed Amanda onto the king-sized bed and began pulling at her garments.

"Whoa! Somebody's in a hurry!" observed Amanda helping with the disrobing.

With no time to waste on small talk, Meatboy got straight to the good stuff. He got inside and began thrusting violently. Paula you bitch, he thought as his orgasm screamed out. He fell back on the bed, winded from his brief but strenuous workout.

Amanda looked up. She wasn't surprised that her client had ejaculated quickly, but she thought he'd last a little longer. She didn't say anything. That would be bad form. She picked up her clothing from the floor and shimmied into her mini skirt. A glint of steel against white flesh caught her attention. "What's the key for?" she asked of the locker key hanging from Meatboy's nipple ring.

"Just a souvenir," muttered Meatboy. He felt cheated and embarrassed.

Amanda began dressing. "So how come you asked for me? Most guys pick Sapphire," she asked, wriggling into her bra.

"No particular reason. How come you ask so many questions?" Meatboy sat on the edge of the bed. He wanted a shot of Jim Beam but didn't want to go out into the living room so soon.

"No need to get nasty. You owe me two hundred dollars." Amanda picked up her handbag and waited expectantly. She charged extra if a client wanted to treat her like shit.

"Wait," said Meatboy jumping up, balls bouncing, "Don't go out there yet!" He pulled on his jeans and yanked a wad of cash from his pocket. Peeling off three hundred dollars, he pressed them into her hand. "Let's talk a bit."

Amanda tucked the money away and sat down beside Meatboy. She understood. "What instrument do you play?" she asked feigning interest.

Meatboy talked for awhile about the thrill of being in a band and how much fun it was to give people tinnitus. Then suddenly he was telling her about Paula and how she frustrated him—it all came pouring out. Abruptly, Meatboy realised that he was baring his soul to a hooker and stopped talking. He felt like an idiot.

Amanda patted his knee comfortingly. Bartenders and hookers were good listeners, it was part of the job.

"It's okay," she assured him. "I know what it's like."

Meatboy and Amanda exited the bedroom. Atlas looked up, his mouth full of steak. Both he and the hooker were fully clothed and appeared to have spent the entire time eating.

"Hi guys!" said Atlas around his food. "Man, this grub is great! You should try some."

"Nice of you to save me a bit," Meatboy quipped sarcastically. He wasn't really hungry anyway. Picking up the Jim Beam, he guzzled directly from the bottle.

Tommy and Heidi reappeared. The bassist wore a satisfied smile, but had lost his T-shirt. Noticing that the food was half gone and Atlas was still eating, he rushed over and snatched the last two steaks off the cart.

"Holy shit, Atlas. You work fast. How did ya manage to get laid and eat all the food!"

Atlas looked up quizzically. "We didn't have sex, I just met this girl! I can't screw somebody I don't even know."

"Yeah! He's a real gentleman," said Sapphire. "I get paid anyway, right?" She refilled her glass with champagne.

"Sure, I don't care," said Meatboy. Out came the roll of bills. Spilling bourbon, he paid all the girls extra. "Get yourselves some new garter belts," he told them.

The girls left smiling, but Meatboy was in a black mood. He began drinking faster and faster. Picking up the last burrito, he whipped it against a wall. It left a trail like a slug and slid greasily to the floor.

"Whatsamatter whichoo?" asked Tommy. He was feeling fine.

"I dunno," said Meatboy morosely. Taking another swill of bourbon he got up and opened one of the large, living room windows.

"Is it warm in here?" asked Tommy. He was beginning to worry about Meatboy.

Meatboy staggered under the weight of the 30" television as he carried it to the window. With a grunt he heaved the appliance into space. The television set imploded with a muffled crump and bounced, twinkling, onto the roof of an adjoining building.

Straightening, Meatboy grinned hugely. "I always wanted to do that," he said. "I feel much better now!"

17

Earl burned like a thousand angry suns. Not only had he been forced to wait until Wednesday for a welfare check, but they had made him jump through hoops of fire to collect one at all. Angrily, he tore the check from the receptionist's hand and stalked raging from the office. Outside on the street, Otis was studying his check.

"How much didya get?" he asked, apprehensive of Earl's fury.

"A hundred and seventy-six fucking bucks! That's forty dollars less than we got five years ago!"

"Well, I guess they're trying to cut back on tramps like us," said Otis philosophically.

"Like fuck!" raged Earl. "They're cutting back on everyone!" He tucked the check into his shirt pocket. "C'mon, lets go cash these suckers and get some booze."

After having their checks shaved down even further by Cash Mart, Otis and Earl purchased a large supply of alcohol at the liquor store. Spotting a taxi, Earl hailed it over.

"Shotgun!" shouted Otis.

Earl grumbled as they loaded the booze into the cab. "You had the front seat last time."

Bad Eddie and his mates were waiting eagerly when Otis and Earl arrived in shantytown.

"Goot ta see ya!" welcomed Bumticker. It would have been good to see the Gestapo if they had brought booze with them.

Earl opened up a bottle of Wild Wedding and passed it around. "Here's to yer health, gentlemen." His bottle returned considerably lighter. He took a mighty belt not to fall behind. Taking a glance around at the assembled N.T.R.A. members, he noticed one was missing.

"What happened to Tornado Jones?" he asked.

"He decided to move on," answered Stovepipe. "He caught a train headed south yesterday." Here today, gone tomorrow.

Earl shrugged, there were still five members left to do the job. "Have any of you guys seen those fuckin' punk rockers around?"

"I saw some at the soup kitchen this morning but I didn't see that big one you were talking about. These guys were all pretty skinny looking, they sure as hell don't scare me." said Stovepipe reaching for the bottle. "So what's our plan?"

"Who needs a plan?" Bad Eddie said confidently. "We'll just go in there and knock 'em around like punching bags!" He opened a bottle of vodka and took a large swizzle.

Otis wished they weren't going to the squat at all, but to voice his disapproval would do nothing to win the respect of his peers. His spirit sank as the sun went behind a cloud bank, and simultaneously he marveled at how the accident could have changed him so profoundly.

At one point in his life, Otis had everything a man could ask for. His career as a bank manager was looking bright. He had an attractive wife, two happy, intelligent children, a spacious new home, a dog, two cars and membership in the local country club. Then one day on his way home from work, a cement truck ran a red light and broadsided his brand new Mercedes. Waking up from a coma, he had undergone months of extensive therapy to regain the use of his arms and legs. Worse yet was his outlook on life—he was angry at the world and he didn't know why. Things that used to be important to him no longer meant a thing. He couldn't understand why he had ever wanted to be a bank manager, have a mortgage, a lawnmower he could drive, taxes, insurance, satellite television with 236 channels of viewing enjoyment. He was thirty-six years old and felt like he had never lived day in his life. His willingness to be just another cog in the machine had been replaced with both an insatiable thirst and a rapidly decreasing concern for consequence. Bewildered by the sudden change in her husband, his wife was at her wits end. The man who had come home from the hospital was not the same man she had married. This one had not gone back to his job at the bank, instead he stayed out all night and came back the next day reeking of booze and stale perfume. He started to get mean, as though it were her fault he was no longer happy. And even when he was home, it was if he were deliberately sailing the leaky boat of their marriage for the rocky shores of divorce. The crack in their marriage became a yawning chasm.

The more Otis drank, the less happy he became with the life of the bourgeoisie. He felt the suburbs pressing in from all sides. He couldn't take it any longer. One day, with only the cash in his wallet and the clothes on his back, he left. Now that was so long ago he barely recalled his wife's name.

Whap! An open handed slap brought him quickly back to the present.

"Wake up, man! What the fuck is the matter with you? Sometimes I could swear you're not really here at all,"

Earl shouted at him. The other tramps shuffled their feet, uncomfortable with the domestic familiarity the newcomers were displaying.

Otis realised he had been taking a short reality break. "None-a your business!" he snapped. "Why the hell are you always getting on my case?" He wasn't sure if life with the N.T.R.A. was what he was after, but he knew that life on the narrow sure wasn't.

Earl curiously watched his partner. He didn't know what Otis was thinking about when he drifted off into wherever it was he went. Over the years he had learned very little about the grumbly little prick, only that he had once had a wife and a job. Not that he really cared, but sometimes he wondered exactly what his partner was running away from. He himself had just been born bad. As a child he enjoyed the usual serial killer pastimes such as lighting cats on fire and beating up his classmates for their lunch money. Earl had never taken time to stop and smell the flowers; he had been too busy stealing hubcaps and selling oregano as marijuana. Strangely, he never thought of himself as a criminal. Breaking the law seemed so natural that he was often unaware he was doing anything wrong. Apprehended at the scene of some mis-deed, he invariably wore a childish, puzzled expression,

"You guys been around each udder too much," observed Bad Eddie. The risk of traveling with a partner was that inevitably he became your surrogate wife. Eddie didn't really give a shit about their problems, and hadn't even decided if he wouldn't rob these new guys when the proper opportunity presented itself. Loyalty amongst N.T.R.A. members wasn't particularly high.

Bumticker rolled a bottle of sherry behind some bushes when the new guys weren't looking. The booze was disappearing fast and undoubtedly the pilfered bottle would come in handy later.

Bad Eddie wanted clarification on the subject of the punk rockers. "So how did you manage to let these dudes get the jump on you? Who started this whole thing?"

Neither Otis nor Earl felt any inclination to be forthcoming on the subject, but Earl decided to take the opportunity to brush up on his lying. "We just happened to jump into the same car they were on, and they bushwhacked us when we weren't looking." He realised after he had spoken that, as far as lies go, this wasn't a good one.

Bad Eddie left it alone; he hadn't expected the truth anyway. Getting to his feet, he brushed off the seat of his jeans and took another snort of whiskey. "Well, we might as well get this thing done before it starts raining. We can take some drinks with us."

This was fine with Earl. He couldn't wait to even the score with those gawddamn punks. Wait till they got a load of Bad Eddie.

Brushing aside requests for booze from other tramps, the gang boiled out of shantytown and began the trek to the squat. Otis paused to lift a bottle and winced. The infection of his shoulder wound was getting worse — it was almost as if the venom and anger he held inside was seeping out through his skin. He had to admit, payback would be sweet. He looked over at Earl talking with Bad Eddie. He didn't trust the surly young gang member. There was something about him that just didn't gel.

Heavy, low clouds had moved in by the time the crew arrived at the squat. No signs of activity were evident; no one seemed to be home. Earl went to the window he had seen being used as a door and looked inside.

Ratty-looking couches and chairs were strewn about haphazardly and garbage thickly carpeted the floor. For a homey touch, posters advertising old punk shows had been tacked to the brick walls with chewing gum. In one corner five or six mattresses lay on the bare concrete floor. It wasn't the Four Seasons hotel by a long stretch.

"It doesn't look like anyone's home," whispered Bad Eddie. "Let's go in and take a look around."

The tramps climbed in through the window. Stovepipe wrinkled his nose in distaste; he liked the smell of his own stench better, but he had to admit that as far as squats went, this was a good one. "At least they have a proper roof," he said. "Maybe we should move in here!"

"You can have it," offered Earl. He was disappointed the punks weren't present.

"Hey!" came a voice from the back of the warehouse. "What the fuck do you guys want?" A tall, scuzzy-looking punker had risen from behind a pile of garbage and didn't look very happy about the intrusion.

"We wanna talk to you!" said Earl walking towards him.

The punk picked up a two-by-four lying on the floor and brandished it threateningly. "That's far enough!" he commanded.

The tramps paid the order no heed and circled around until they had the punk loosely surrounded. "No need for the stick, son. We just wanna ask you a couple of questions," said Bad Eddie.

Earl took over. "Have you seen three punkers around here, one of 'ems real big, and another one has green hair."

The punker's girlfriend sat up in her sleeping bag. "Nope, ain't seen nobody like that."

"Yeah, hit the fuckin' road. This is private property!"
The punk took a test swing with the two-by-four. Before
he could get it back into a striking position, Bad Eddie
lunged forward and knocked the club from his hand.
Slamming the punk to the concrete, he got a forearm
across his victim's windpipe and slapped the kid. Hard.

"I'm gonna ask you again. Where can we find those
guys?"

"I'm telling you," choked the punk "We don't know!"

Without warning, the punk's girlfriend jumped on
Bad Eddie's back and began pulling his greasy hair. "Let
him go, you filthy bastard!" she shrieked, trying to get
her fingers into his eyes.

"YOWCH!" hollered Bad Eddie. "Somebody get this
bitch offa me!"

Earl and Stovepipe rushed over and pulled the girl off.
With malnourished muscles and a great deal of effort, they
managed to restrain the wildly struggling female.

"Ya gotta watch out fer their wimmin," warned Otis.
"They hit hard."

The male punker, freed by his girlfriend's actions,
charged the tramps with both arms swinging. It was a
chivalrous thing to do, but stupid. Stovepipe and Earl
tackled and held him while Bad Eddie nailed him in the
stomach. The punk grunted as the blows knocked the
wind from him.

"Lemme go, you fuggin' pricks," choked the pint-
sized punk. Thrashing wildly, he broke free and made it
back to the window before he was once again tackled and
brought back under submission. Lifting their victim to
his feet, Bumticker held his arms while Otis pummeled
his chest and ribs, the muffled blows thudding hollowly
in the empty warehouse.

"Where are they?" interrogated Otis. The beating continued but now the punches were directed towards the victim's face, his head snapping back and forth, blood streaming down his face in crimson rivers.

"Leave him alone you fuckin' jerks!" yelled the punkette. "Those guys you're after have a warehouse over on Glen Street by Hastings!" She couldn't stand by and watch the beating any longer.

Otis and Stovepipe released their victim who slid limply to the floor.

"What's the address?" Bad Eddie asked calmly.

"I don't know!" shrieked the girl, "We haven't been there yet!"

Earl picked up the two by four and smacked the little punk just for good measure. "Let's go have some drinks. We should be able to find them easy enough now."

18

"Let's take that last track from the top," came the producer's mechanical voice from inside the sound booth.

"Why?" asked Meatboy, "It sounded fine to me." The band had already played the song eight times in a row. How good did it have to be? It was, after all, punk. None of the band members had ever been in a recording studio before and hadn't expected it to be this much work.

Atlas, however, trusted the producer. "C'mon, let's just play the song. Once more can't hurt!"

Meatboy tried to summon the strength for another full-out attack. It was hard to give a song one hundred and ten percent if you knew you were just going to repeat it over and over. Taking a slug of beer, he nodded his readiness to the band.

Tommy barked into the mike, "1-2-3-4!"

The band fell into the song like a cement truck with no brakes. If anything, the country accent merely added to the "Hillbillies on Speed" debauchery of the tune. If the band was suffering any side effects from the week-long binge, it was not apparent. The kick drum snapped like a wet sheet on a windy day as Tommy and the Rat thumped out the rhythm. Meatboy thrashed the mike stand as he belted out the vocals.

When mama died, the bank foreclosed on the farm.
I caught my hand in an auger and lost half my arm.

Then the pigs all died and the house burnt down.
I could hear the bank laughing, all the way from town.

I got them cowpoke blues, what am I gonna do?
Guess I'll move to the city, got nothing left to lose.

As Atlas busted into the lead a guitar string snapped, throwing his guitar out of tune. Meatboy rolled his eyes in disgust and threw down his mike stand. The band stumbled to a halt.

"Fuck!" yelled Meatboy. "Now we gotta do the song again?" Patience was not one of his strong points.

"No, that was fine!" came the voice from the sound booth. "We'll mix in the lead from another track. I think we have enough on that song, let's move on to something else." Either the producer had all he needed, or he was as tired as the band was.

"Hell, let's take five," said Tommy unslinging his bass. His throat felt like the Sahara. He picked up a pitcher of ice water and drank half of it, pouring the rest over his head. Reeling and dizzy, he joined his mates in the lounge area. Now that they were offstage, Fire in the Hole looked more like Mud in the Basement. None of them had slept much since Meatboy had stumbled into their lives, and no rest was in sight.

"What's next?" asked Atlas. Of the group, he was the only one who didn't look like he'd been put through the tumble cycle in an industrial dryer.

"Let's get a couple more tracks down and we'll call it a day," said Meatboy popping a can of beer. If he stopped drinking now, he would turn into a bag of shit. Only the alcohol was keeping him going.

It had been no easy job finding a recording studio worth its salt on such short notice but, as usual, money had made it happen. Meatboy figured at the rate he was spending this single might be the only thing he had to show for his incredible find.

Tommy struggled to his feet. "C'mon, let's get this thang done!" He wanted to go back to the warehouse and sleep for seventy-two hours.

The rest of the group dragged themselves, exhausted, back to the sound stage. After interminable tuning, they were as ready as they could be.

"Let's try 'Psycho Bitch'," suggested Meatboy. It was a new song Atlas and he had just written but that still needed work.

The Rat tried to sit down behind his drum kit but lost his footing and tumbled directly into the set. Cymbal stands and tom-toms crashed to the floor in a noisy tangle. The Rat lay sprawled among the scattered pieces of his kit.

"Somebody, help me up!" said the drummer feebly reaching out his hand.

Atlas hauled the drummer to his feet. The Rat looked like he was ready to fall again, but Atlas kept his grip on the drummer's shoulder to prevent him.

"Maybe we should just call it a day," suggested Tommy. He was beginning to lose the feeling in his fingertips.

"If you sissies can't handle it, let's pack it in," said Meatboy. He was privately relieved the recording session was over.

The producer came out from his seat in the sound booth. He was a bright-eyed, intense young man with rapid, jerky movements. "I think I've got enough to produce a solid version of 'Cowpoke Blues'. Do you mind if I play it for a couple of people I know in the industry? It's different-sounding. I like it!"

Meatboy wasn't paying attention. "Sure, knock yourself out. I'll phone you to book some more time next week." He didn't even know what he was going to do with the singles once he had them pressed; he just wanted them.

The group was quiet as they piled into Meatboy's car. The sun was shining and the top was down, but everyone was too beat to pay any attention to the weather.

"Maybe we could rest up tonight and have a party tomorrow," suggested Meatboy, batteries fading fast.

"Yeah!" enthused Atlas, "Then we'll have a chance to play!"

"Might even make some money," said the Rat who had managed to stay awake. While he was appreciative of Meatboy's generosity, he was not entirely comfortable with it. He would be much happier if he could earn his own money.

"Sounds like a plan to me," agreed Tommy.

Paula and Silvi were sleeping when the boys got back. Meatboy went straight to the fridge and grabbed a beer. Utterly exhausted, he flung himself onto an unoccupied couch.

"You're back," Paula said drowsily.

"Urrrgghh!" replied Meatboy. Seconds later, he was asleep.

Leo had covered the whole area a dozen times and was still no closer to finding the elusive punk. Local street people claimed to have seen him recently, but none would say where he lived. Leo, however, was becoming ever more popular. When junkies and winos saw him coming their faces would light up with big, toothless smiles.

"Good morning Leo," they would say. "Do you happen to have any spare change on you?" And even though Leo knew they had no useful information, he would invariably dig into his pockets and come up with a few loose coins. Today was no exception. As he stepped out of a corner store, a panhandler he knew well beckoned him over. Leo could see the bum was in a state of high agitation, his bony shoulders shook as he spoke.

"I seen dat guy you were lookin' for yesterday! He was with some other punk rockers!" In his excitement, the panhandler had neglected to ask for any money up front.

"Where?" Leo wanted to know. By now, he had pretty much given up any hope of finding the missing loot but was still going through the motions.

"Just down the road aways on Glen Drive!" Suddenly the informant remembered his need for remuneration. His eyes gleamed as he thought about the crack he would soon be smoking. "I can show you where he lives for a small fee."

"How much?" asked Leo. He was still pessimistic about the situation.

The bum did some fast calculating in his head. "I'd say twenny bucks is about right." He eyed Leo cautiously, hoping he hadn't overestimated the value of the information.

Leo sighed and fished out his wallet. Inspecting its contents, he selected a ten dollar bill and proffered it to the slavering informant. "Ten bucks down, ten when I see the place."

The bill quickly disappeared into one of the bum's many pockets. "Dis way!" he said, and immediately stepped out onto Commercial Drive causing a psychedelic vw micro-bus to slam on its brakes. The hippie behind the wheel waited indulgently for the pair to cross. He knew that jaywalking on the Drive was a local tradition.

The bum must have been in a hurry to collect the other half of his fee, for he set off down the street at a fair clip. Leo had to rush to keep up. Presently, they came to a dank, little used alley.

"It's just 'round the corner," motioned the frail panhandler.

A row of abandoned loading docks and boarded up windows overlooked the cracked concrete of the lane. A startled cat darted out of nowhere and disappeared into a tiny chink between two buildings. Outside a dilapidated warehouse stood a canary yellow '64 Parisienne Custom ragtop.

"I think that's their car," said the panhandler looking around to make sure there were no witnesses to his indiscretion.

A door opened and two girls emerged from the warehouse. Leo couldn't understand why people would want to dress in such a manner. When clothes were torn they should be thrown away. It was all so…uncivilized. One of the girls, a blonde with a red, latex miniskirt, ripped stockings, and abundant chains and earrings, glanced at them suspiciously.

"You guys looking for something?" Silvi asked warily.

Leo was nonplused; he hadn't been expecting a direct confrontation just yet. "Uh, no. We're just passing through." The bum shrank back—he had no desire to become involved.

The blonde's dark-haired companion stared at them with equal distrust. "C'mon Silvi, let's go." She walked towards the opposite end of the alley, her muscled haunches rolling athletically under the tight leather of her jeans. The blonde gave Leo and the bum a final squint and hurried to catch up with her friend.

The panhandler was anxious to collect his fee and depart. "Them's their girlfriends. Now gimme my money!"

Leo paid the bum, who quickly turned and scurried away. Leaving the alley, Leo walked back up to Commercial Drive and into the closest coffee shop. Ordering a mocha with extra chocolate sprinkles, he pulled out his phone and called Whitney.

"Hello?" answered the politician with a slight tremor in his voice.

"Hi, Whitney. It's me. I've got good news!"

Anxiety turned to exasperation. "Well, what is it?"

Leo wished Whitney didn't have to be so abrupt. "I've found out where the punk rocker lives. What do you want me to do now?"

A pause. Whitney hadn't really thought this far ahead. "That's good. That's real good. Don't do anything for now. I'll call you back when I'm ready to move." He hadn't expected Leo to actually track the thief down.

"When will I see you?"

"I'll call you soon," said Whitney hanging up. He needed time to think.

All week he had been pressuring everyone even remotely connected with the Skytrain expansion for a final decision. He had also been working closely with city planners trying to find a suitable route, but so far nothing had been decided. To make matters worse, Braden's phone calls for information came with thinly veiled threats. In the last call he'd been extremely cliché, mentioning both overshoes and cement in the same sentence. Whitney wished he could trust Braden to help collect the money, but at this point he didn't trust the mobster not to just keep whatever was left of the money. Truly, a nail-biter.

It was already past noon. Whitney had been so busy trying to cover his ass he hadn't even had time to step out for his usual three martini lunch. He reached into his desk drawer for the bottle he kept for emergencies. Taking a large bite of the intoxicating potato, he wiped his mouth and thought out his alternatives. As much as he hated to think about it, he had to accept the fact that he might have to collect the money himself. Leo certainly wouldn't be much help in the muscle department. Steeling his resolve, Whitney unlocked the bottom drawer of his desk. Shoving aside the useless portfolio he had compiled for Braden, he removed a .38 police special and a box of ammunition. Acquiring a pistol and a license hadn't been difficult for a man of the Minister's position. It was ostensibly for protection.

Loading the pistol, Whitney wondered why money was so important to him. But then he remebered that money was power; and power, of course, was what it was all about. Now with a loaded gun in his hand, he was determined to let nothing get in his way. He buckled an ankle holster to his leg and tucked the pistol into it. There was no time left for reflection.

Without a glance at his secretary, he got into the elevator and took it down to the parkade. Easing the big Mercedes into traffic, he pulled out his phone and speed-dialed Leo's number. He had decided that now would be the best time to address this problem. Stopping at a red light, he waited impatiently until Leo answered.

"Sorry, Whitney. I couldn't hear the phone for the traffic," apologized his assistant.

"Never mind!" snapped Whitney. "I want you to meet me—what the hell?"

Two men wearing business suits climbed into Whitney's car at the red light. One of them forced Whitney over in the seat and took the wheel; the other hijacker held a nasty-looking gun on the Minister just below the level of the dashboard. Reaching over, he took the phone from Whitney's numb fingers and pressed END.

"What the bloody jesus is the meaning of this?" asked Whitney in his most outraged voice, although he had a good idea what it was about.

"Just shaddup. Braden wants to talk to you," said the uninvited guest in the passenger seat.

"But, but..." Whitney sputtered to a halt.

The driver dodged in and out of traffic expertly. Leaving downtown via the Granville St. Bridge, he took the Fir Ave. exit and traveled quickly to a modest, but tasteful brick tudor on West 10th. Activating the garage door, the driver drove inside and parked the car. Whitney was quickly ushered into a cozy den where Braden was waiting by the fire.

"So glad you could make it, Whitney," said Braden looking up from his brandy snifter.

"You could have phoned me, you know." Whitney brushed himself off and tried not to let his terror show.

"Sure I could have," Braden agreed affably. "But you have to admit this is a much more effective way to get my point across."

"I thought I already explained to you about the difficulties I ran into."

"I'm tired of your excuses. I want results, and I want them now!" Braden's congenial attitude was gone. He stared at Whitney with murder in his eye.

Whitney thought desperately for a way to stall for more time. "We still haven't resolved our problems, but I did find the guy who snatched the money."

"You mean my money," corrected Braden, "And I still don't have anything to show for it." The crime boss thought for a moment. "Where is my money?"

Whitney hesitated. He didn't know either. "My assistant has the address. I was just on my way to meet him when your goons grabbed me."

"My boys will accompany you to collect the money, then we'll talk further."

Whitney opened his mouth to protest, but Braden lifted a hand cutting him off. "Don't give me any more bullshit, I don't even vote. Just get outta here and pray for your balls that things go smoothly."

The politician wisely elected not to say anything further and followed Braden's goons back out to his car. This time he was allowed to sit in the passenger seat, while one goon drove and the other sat in the back.

"Where to?" asked the driver. He was an ugly man with small, piggish eyes and a sloping, oily forehead.

Whitney was petulant and uncooperative. "How much does Braden pay you guys, anyway?"

"Never mind the questions," said the goon in the back. "Just tell us where yer supposed to hook up with yer buddy."

"I'd be surprised if that cheapskate gives you more than ten bucks an hour," speculated Whitney. "I could do a whole lot better than that."

The driver was beginning to tire of the politician's patronizing attitude. "What difference does it make to you how much we make. Anything would be better than working for a slug like you!" The trio were rolling east on Broadway towards Main St, still aimless.

"Tut, tut," chided Whitney in his most condescending tone. "I was just about to suggest that we share any money recovered. You boys are such lowly-paid lackeys, I figured you could use a raise." He had no intention of doing any such thing and was just stalling for time until he could think of a way out of this mess.

Now Jimmy was really starting to lose it. "Shut the fuck up and tell us where we're supposed to be going!" Half turning in his seat, he grabbed Whitney by the lapels and began shaking him violently.

"Hey! Watch where yer goin'!" shouted Freddy from the back.

Jimmy released the insolent politician and refocused his attention on the road a fraction of a second too late. Wheels locked, the Mercedes slid screeching through an intersection and plowed into the rear side panel of a red Dodge Dart. Fortunately for Whitney, Jimmy hit the windshield just before he did, leaving a jagged hole for him to slingshot into the street. The driver, prevented from sailing out of the car by the steering wheel, flew back into his seat as his companion piled over him and out onto the hood of the car. The other vehicle spun around crazily and snapped off a fire hydrant, sending a thick column of water into the air. It was swingtime in whiplash city. Whitney had no time to even register the impact as he soared through the stratosphere and landed on the boulevard in an iridescent shower of auto glass. Dazed and wondering if he was still alive, Whitney looked up at the sky and marveled at how bright and shiny everything looked. It was funny how going from 60 km to zero in no seconds flat could make you appreciate your next breath.

All was vacuum quiet.

The sound came rushing back in as Whitney slowly sat up and surveyed the scene. The Mercedes had come to rest against a light standard, the driver slumped bleeding over the wheel, his barrel-chest engaging the horn. Screaming pedestrians, the whoosh of water from the fire hydrant, and the distant whine of police sirens all fought for dominance in this nightmarish tableau. A shocked-looking teenage girl approached Whitney slowly.

"Are you okay, Mister?"

Whitney got shakily to his feet and dusted himself off. His ears were ringing and he could feel the fingers of his left hand swelling, but considering that all his limbs were still attached to his torso, he felt very fortunate indeed. The world pounding in his head, he stumbled away.

19

Word of a party travels fast in East Vancouver, especially if you spend the day on the street drinking beer and handing out photocopied flyers announcing the event. Paula had enticed local punkers Kraft Dinner Revenge and a new group called Sickbee Three to round out the itinerary. Fire in the Hole would be headlining. After all, it was their warehouse. The flyers, carefully lettered by Atlas and printed on snot-green paper, were now strewn from one end of Commercial Drive to the other. All the members of Fire in the Hole bustled about the warehouse in preparation for the evening's festivities. Meatboy had a table set up by the back door and eagerly awaited the first arrivals.

"Ya think anybody is going to show up?" he asked Paula, looking for affirmation.

"Probably," responded Paula, "Kraft Dinner Revenge are pretty well known, they're bound to attract a few people. I had to promise them free beer and fifty bucks." She sat down on a folding aluminum chair and rested her head in her hands. Work had been hellish today. The travel agency was exceptionally busy with people of all description booking passage for flights all over the globe. How did they manage to save enough money to go anywhere? Instead of planning a trip here she was, volunteering her services to help get this gig together. Paula wasn't quite sure why. She lifted a can of beer to her green-lipsticked lips and took a hefty swallow.

A van pulled up and a group of scruffy young punks clambered out.

"We're Sickbee Three," said the driver. "Where's the beer?"

Meatboy jerked a thumb towards the back of the hall. "In the back. There's a fridge full of beer and a room where you can stow yer gear. If you're Sickbee Three, how come there's four of you?"

One of the group, a pudgy little guy with an angry red face and a bristly haircut gave Meatboy a "what kind of an idiot are you?" look. "I don't think Sickbee Four has the same ring to it, do you?" he said in a truculent manner.

"Guess not," admitted Meatboy.

The group unloaded their equipment and began setting up. Paula went into the bathroom to take a pee. On the cubicle door some street poet had scrawled a verse in felt pen:

I'M THE BUG
Sticky bits and pieces of your last meal
coat my legs and abdomen
Thank you for providing me with such a tasty snack
Spill me some beer
Try not to step on me with your big clumsy foot
You can wipe me out, but I've laid eggs.

Hovering over the bowl, eyes peeled for cockroaches, she noticed—without surprise—that there was no toilet paper. She should have known. Reluctantly, she settled for the old, drip-dry method and got the hell out of the stinking cubicle. One urinal and one bowl for two-hundred-plus people. That should be just fine.

Meatboy stumbled into the bathroom and knocked Paula from her reverie.

"Oops, sorry, I didn't know you were in here," he apologized. For all his bluster and punk swagger, he couldn't escape the fact that his parents had brought him up to respect the privacy of others. He tried to cover his embarrassment with impertinence. "Don't let me stop ya, just go about your business. I've seen your pussy before, ya know."

Paula casually brushed aside this bit of rudeness. "Dream on, Meathead. I'm all done. By the way, you might wanna spring for a couple rolls of asswipe, or can't you afford it?"

Offended by this cheap shot, he pulled out a double and stuffed it into Paula's hand. "You go get the paper if yer so worried about it." He stepped up to the urinal and unzipped. "Keep the change," he added over his shoulder.

"Fuck you," said Paula angrily. "You can't buy everybody, ya know. I'm not some tart you can order up in a fancy hotel." She crumpled the twenty dollar bill into a ball and tossed it at Meatboy's back. For all her toughness, she was hurt that Meatboy had resorted to prostitutes.

Meatboy was flabbergasted. How did Paula know about the hookers? One of those bigmouths must have spilled the beans. He finished up and left the washroom. Someone needed a kick in the arse.

Onstage Sickbee Three were conducting a noisy sound check. The angry-faced kid was the singer/guitarist. He stepped up to the mike.

"Check! Testing!" His amplified voice boomed across the empty warehouse with sonic intensity.

Meatboy kept going. There were several small offices in the back, the larger of which had been converted into a bar. The Rat sat on a stool nursing a beer.

"You ready to kick some ass tonight?" asked the drummer, taking a conservative hit of malt.

"I'm ready to kick some ass right now!" steamed Meatboy. "How did Paula find out about those hookers?"

"I dunno," shrugged the Rat. "I didn't even see them. By the way, thanks for saving me one."

"Ya snooze, ya loose," Meatboy reminded him. "Where's Tommy?"

The Rat cast his eyes up at the ceiling. "Upstairs."

With no further questions, Meatboy climbed the steep flight of stairs to the loft above. In the gloom, he could make out two sweaty, naked bodies on a mattress in the corner. The Rat hadn't told him Tommy had company.

"What the fuck do you want?" cursed Tommy.

"Oops, sorry," said Meatboy for the second time that evening. "I wanted to ask you something, but it can wait."

"Well then you won't mind if I ask you to *get the fuck outta here!*"

"Huh? Oh yeah, sorry," he apologized again. He realised he had been staring at Silvi's swollen nipples. Embarrassed again, he scurried down the stairs, gently shutting the door at the bottom.

The first guests had arrived and were arguing with Atlas at the door.

"We're the Jaks!" insisted one of the skaters. "Why aren't we on the guest list? We never have to pay!"

"I don't know about no Jaks," Atlas maintained doggedly, "The cover charge is three bucks."

Paula brushed past Meatboy before he had a chance to get involved. "It's okay, Atlas. Let them in."

Atlas shrugged and waved the skate team past. Once inside, the skaters jumped on their boards and began shredding the hall.

"Who's the Jaks?" asked Meatboy. "And how come they don't have to pay?"

"They're *the* East Van skate team. It's simpler to have them on your side than against you. Besides, they drink their own weight in beer. We still make money offa them."

"Bunch freeloaders, ya ask me," grumbled Meatboy under his breath.

Atlas was more concerned with logistics. "How can they skate when they're drunk?" he wondered. "I tried it once and ran into a police car."

More punks began to arrive and Paula knew them all personally. "Hey, Chris and Christine! Long time no see! I guess you found a babysitter, huh."

"Yeah. We talked Denise into it. We had to leave her a six-pack," grumbled Chris. He couldn't understand why his friends wouldn't just babysit for free.

"C'mon in! The bar's in the back."

Christine held out some money but Paula refused to accept it. "Forget it, you can buy me a beer sometime."

"Don't anybody have to pay?" demanded Meatboy after they had passed.

"My friends are all on the guest list," said Paula defensively. "This way, if I run outta beer someday, hopefully they'll remember I did them a favour."

"Don't help me none," complained Meatboy. He was constantly forgetting he didn't have to worry about money matters anymore.

Guests began arriving in droves. Paula had taken over at the door and continued to let her friends in for free, greeting them all warmly. "Meatboy, this is Matt and Jen, Sourpuss, Ash, René, Noel, Francine, Scottish John, Ramona, Martin, Sideshow Tim, Josianne, Greg What, Otis and Cassandra, PLB, Bruno, and Chris Gonish," Paula said breathlessly.

Meatboy shook hands and did his best to play host. He wasn't very good at remembering names, unless they belonged to pretty girls. Still, he was happy about the large numbers arriving. After tonight, all the punks in the city would be talking about this show. He was as nervous as a cop at a forum on police brutality and hoped the band wasn't getting too drunk. Especially the Rat— he had a tendency to fall off his drum stool when he was really hammered.

Sickbee Three took the stage and opened their set with what sounded like some kind of crappy 90's dance music. They were halfway through the first song before Meatboy realised they were covering a Black Flag number:

> Sitting here like a loaded gun, waiting to go off
> I've got nothing better to do but shoot my mouth off
> So gimme, gimme, gimme/I need some more
> Gimme, gimme, gimme/Don't ask what for

Meatboy couldn't believe what they were doing to the song. This was blasphemy! No, no, no! he wanted to shout. This ain't no disco! Apparently the crowd was none too fond of the rendition either; they began pelting the band with beer cans and booing loudly. Sickbee Three abruptly shifted gears and began slamming out the power chords. With a noise not unlike an automobile manufacturing plant in full production, they brutalized their instruments with savage glee. The fans who had been calling for blood seconds earlier began moshing their brains out. The first song had merely been a joke to catch everyone off guard.

Meatboy laughed and pushed his way to the front of the stage. These guys weren't too bad after all. If the band wasn't hitting all the right notes, it was because they were bouncing around like jack-in-the-boxes on methamphetamine. In a frenzy, the bass player pounded out the last note of the last song and threw his guitar into the air. Unfortunately the instrument landed the wrong way, the neck snapping with a unique and disturbing sound similar to a piano on the end of a broken bungee chord. Heartbrokenly, the guitar flinger cradled his shattered instrument in his arms. The crowd cheered wildly.

Meatboy fought his way back through the sweaty throng to see how things were going at the door. Atlas stood barring the way of four drunken jocks.

"C'mon, man! We just wanna party!"

"Party's full, we already got too many people," Paula said firmly.

"Then a couple more won't matter!" persisted the jock.

"You heard her," Atlas warned meaningfully. "Beat it!"

Reluctantly, the group backed away muttering dire consequences.

"Jumpin' Jello Biafra!" Meatboy said wonderingly. "How many people are here?"

"Too many. I'm trying not to let anybody else in, but it's hard to turn your friends away," complained Paula. Tiny stress lines were visible around her eyes.

"Fuck it! Tell people once they leave they can't come back in," Meatboy said righteously.

Paula stood up from behind the table and shoved the cash box into his chest. "You tell 'em. I'm going to go get some toilet paper and some fresh air." And with that, she fumed out the door into the night.

Atlas looked over quizzically but remained silent.

Meatboy let out a long sigh and plunked himself into a chair. "Women!" he said with agitation. "Can't live with 'em, can't make guitar strings outta their intestines."

Otis had come to the conclusion that Bad Eddie was one cheap son-of-a-bitch. He and Earl had been following the burly train tramp around all day and despite assurances that there would be plenty to drink, they had yet to see more than several small shots of cheap whisky.

"Where are we going now?" he asked moodily. "I'm thirsty."

"A guy up here owes me some bread, if he pays up I'll buy a jug."

Otis and Earl grumbled unhappily but continued to tag along on the off chance that Bad Eddie would make good on his promises. They walked down First Ave. and onto Commercial Drive, stopping for a red light. A snot-green poster taped to a mailbox caught Earl's attention.

"Punk party? Glen Drive? Hey! Lookit this! I wonder if this is where those punkers are staying?"

Otis groaned inwardly. Why couldn't Earl just forget about it? "So what? Those guys aren't going to help our booze situation any. Besides, there'll probably be hundreds of those dayglo motherfuckers there."

Bad Eddie didn't seem too keen on the plan either. "Let's go see if I can collect my money first, then maybe we'll check it out."

Surprisingly they were able to collect ten dollars from Bad Eddie's debtor, likely because of Eddies' hint that without funds they would be forced to hang around all night drinking his booze, watching his television and flirting with his fat, ugly girlfriend. With this tiny dividend and a little extra panhandled change, they were able to purchase two bottles of Andre's Medium Dry Sherry, which they drank straight from the paper bag. Otis thought they were walking aimlessly, but eventually Eddie came to a stop at the entrance to a dingy, narrow alley.

"Why are we stopping?" asked Otis apprehensively.

"Those punker buddies of yours must live on this block somewhere. I thought you wanted to pay them a visit." Bad Eddie wanted to prove he wasn't afraid of no skinny punk rockers.

Conversely, Earl wasn't all that eager to make an appearance without more backup. "How are we gonna get at those guys if all their buddies are hanging around?"

Bad Eddie seemed unconcerned. "If it's a big party they might not notice us, maybe we can sneak in and drink all their booze."

"Sure, what have we got to lose?" replied Earl, thinking nostalgically about his few remaining teeth.

Finding the party was no problem — they followed the sound of distorted guitars to the door of a dumpy warehouse. As they approached, they spotted a group of surly high school jocks getting into a station wagon. Bad Eddie banged heavily on the steel door.

"Good luck!" called one of the jocks from the car. "Those jerks aren't letting anybody else in."

Bad Eddie wanted to see for himself. When no answer came he pounded on the door even more forcefully. Finally, they heard a bolt being thrown back and the door was flung open. Atlas and Meatboy stood blocking the threshold, arms folded on their chests.

"You guys!" exclaimed Meatboy.

The train tramps were also startled. They hadn't expected to see their punk enemies so soon.

Earl recovered first. "Let us in, we just wanna talk to you guys!" he said looking back to Bad Eddie for support.

He noticed that the large hobo had stepped back and was looking at Atlas with an expression akin to fear.

"I don't like you guys!" rumbled Atlas. "Piss off!"

"We just wanna talk!" Earl repeated. Punks were starting to crowd around like spectators at a car wreck.

"Maybe we should come back later," suggested Bad Eddie. He had no stomach for these odds.

"Don't come back at all!" said Meatboy slamming the door in their faces.

"I told you that guy was big!" Otis chortled triumphantly. Bad Eddie wasn't so tough.

Earl looked at Bad Eddie disgustedly. "Well, you were sure a big help."

"You saw how many of them there were! What was I supposed to do?"

Earl didn't bother to respond. He was beginning to suspect that the trash-talking train tramp was probably his own PR man. He uncapped a bottle of sherry and spilled a large portion into his stomach.

"We might as well go back to camp," he said resignedly.

"Gimme some a dat!" demanded Otis.

The tramps made their way down the alley. As they reached the corner, Otis collided with a man headed in the opposite direction. The bottle of sherry jumped from his hand and exploded on the concrete.

"Watch where yer goin' you stupid fuck! Look what you made me do!"

"I'm terribly sorry!" gushed Leo. "I didn't see you coming!"

"Fat lot of good that does me! You owe me six bucks!"

"That bottle was almost empty. I'll give you two bucks," negotiated Whitney, jumping in. It was his nature to squabble over every penny. He fished a two-dollar coin from his pocket and handed it to the hobo.

Bad Eddie scrutinized the newcomers. These guys were peas from two totally different pods. The older one was dressed in a charcoal gray business suit and sported a variety of minor cuts and abrasions, while the younger man looked silly in a brand new T-shirt and spotless, neatly pressed blue jeans. "What are you guys doing here anyway?" he asked curiously.

"I don't see how it's any of your concern," said Whitney attempting to pass. Bad Eddie blocked his path.

"We're going to a punk gig," volunteered Leo nervously. "Do you know where it is?"

Earl looked doubtfully at the pair. "What do you guys want thar?"

It was Whitney's instinct to be evasive, but on further consideration he felt he might be able to use these hooligans. Their requirements were probably minimal. They wouldn't look out of place with DIRTY DEEDS DONE DIRT CHEAP signs hanging around their necks.

"We're looking for somebody, a punk with green hair and black leather jacket with an upside down Canadian flag on the back. You seen him?"

The tramps looked at each other in disbelief.

"Maybe," Earl replied cautiously. "Why? What'd he do to you?"

"He has something that belongs to me. I'll give you guys ten bucks each if you can take me to him and watch my back."

"You're gonna have to make it a little sweeter than that," replied Bad Eddie negatively. "There's a lot of those ugly-looking suckers in there."

As Whitney prepared to counter-offer, a black-garbed punkette carrying a plastic bag hurried past them in the direction of the warehouse.

"Hey!" exclaimed Earl. "That's one a them bitches now!"

"Is she a friend of the green haired guy?" asked Whitney. With unusual speed for a politician, an evil plan began to form in his head. It was traditional for any government employee to form evil plans slowly.

"Yeah! Let's grab her!" said Bad Eddie looking for a safe way to cover his yellow streak.

Whether Paula recognized the train tramps or had just overheard their conversation was unclear. She picked up her heels and made a dash for the warehouse discarding the bag of toilet paper. Bad Eddie and Earl sprinted after her.

Leo was mortified; he wanted absolutely no part of this. "Let's get out of here, Whitney! These guys are bad news!"

One part of Whitney told him to listen to his assistant, but then again if he had the girl, it would certainly give him leverage. Desperately, he racked his brain for the right decision.

Earl and Bad Eddie obviously didn't think that far ahead. They caught up to Paula at the back door of the warehouse. She had time to kick the door once before the tramps pounced on her. Eddie clamped a hand over her mouth as Earl grabbed her savagely kicking legs. They lifted her into the air and carried her back towards the other villains. Paula twisted and squirmed like ten cats in a bag, but her captors managed to maintain a firm grip.

"Get the car," barked Whitney. They would hold the girl hostage. It was too late to do anything else. Stunned, Leo left to do as he was told on the double.

20

Despite his best intentions, Meatboy was fairly shit-faced by the time Fire in the Hole hit the stage. The fans were feeling no pain either, beer cans flew threw the air like large aluminum insects and boisterous laughter filled the hall. Fortunately the Rat hadn't consumed so much alcohol that his perch on the drum stool was unsteady. Atlas, of course, was sober as a judge and eager to get started. He turned up the volume on his Marshall stack evoking a dirty look from the soundman who had already set the sound as loud as he could without massive feedback. Tommy casually sauntered onto the stage and plugged in his bass guitar — it was hard to tell what kind of shape he was in, dark sunglasses hid his eyes from the world.

Meatboy stumbled over and grabbed the microphone. "Good evening, ladies and germs, I hope you're as drunk as I am. This song's for Paula, it's called 'Psycho Bitch'. Hit it Tommy!"

"1-2-3-4!"

Thundering, full-tilt punk blasted from the P.A. columns as Fire in the Hole launched a nuclear warhead into the crowd. Already sweaty and dazed from the pounding Kraft Dinner Revenge had given them, the kids in the pit climbed over each other like rats in a cage. Mayhem ruled supreme under the guns of guitar.

It was slam time.

Well, here she comes walking down the street
She's struttin' around like a cat in heat
If she's not causing trouble, then she's raising hell
With a psycho bitch, you can never tell

The nervousness Meatboy had intended to undo with alcohol dissipated entirely as the band clicked like a well-oiled machine. Dodging a stage-diver, he stepped into the next song without missing a beat. An empty beer can bounced off of his chest. Fools. Didn't they know he was impervious to the harmful intentions of mere mortals? They were lucky he was a benevolent god. Reaching into his jacket pocket, he pulled out a huge handful of five dollar bills and threw money down at his subjects. The time was right to usher in a new era of prosperity.

At first the frenzied mob didn't realise what Meatboy was throwing at them. When they did figure it out, they reacted with understandable enthusiasm. Clawing and shoving they trampled their comrades like K-Mart shoppers on $1.44 day. The temperature on the stage was reaching a hundred degrees as Meatboy removed his leather jacket and shook it over the crowd. Five dollar bills floated down like manna from heaven. The fans went ballistic as they attempted to snatch the fluttering cash from the air.

The rest of the band gaped at Meatboy, stupefied, but continued to play without dropping the beat. What was the point of charging money for a cover if they were just going to give it all away? They finished the song with a deafening crash.

"I just wanna tell you guys," said Meatboy, voice distorted with feedback, "that under no circumstances should any of this money be spent on liquor or drugs!"

"Yeah, right," mocked Tommy stepping up to his microphone.

The crowd responded with shrieks of delight, laughter, jeers and a shower of beer cans. Meatboy scanned the audience for Paula. He had been hoping she would be right up front teaching slam-dance lessons to anyone stupid enough to get in her way, yet she was nowhere to be seen. Was she so mad at him she had gone home? Still, he had a show to do. He nodded to Atlas who began the guitar intro to "Cowpoke Blues". The rest of the band fell into the song as Meatboy slammed out the vocals, veins popping on his forehead. Stage divers lined up for the privilege of hurtling themselves onto the writhing mass below. Unless the diver was really popular, the dancers would move out of the way, allowing the unfortunate sap to hit the floor like a sack of dirt. Broken bones, bruises and bloody noses were the order of the day. All in good fun.

Drenched in sweat and feeling a deep exhaustion creep into their bones, Fire in the Hole finished their set to riotous applause. As the Rat stood up to depart he tumbled forward, nearly impaling himself on the hi-hat. Overcompensating, he lurched sideways and fell over the bass drum. Dislodged microphones screeched out a steady high-pitched squeal until the soundman mercifully shut them off at the board. The fans screamed their approval—they thought it was part of the act. Meatboy picked up his leather jacket and stepped down from the stage. Atlas slapped a huge hand on his shoulder.

"Good job, man. How come you didn't tell us you were gonna give out all that money? That was great!" he asked wiping the sweat from his face with the bottom of his T-shirt.

"What, and spoil the surprise? Hey listen, have you seen Paula?"

"No, I haven't seen her since we started playing."

"Me neither," said Meatboy shaking his head. "Listen, I gotta go find her. I'll see ya later." Shaking hands with members of the audience, he made his way through the crowd to the back door.

Silvi stood up when she saw him coming. "Meatboy! Where's Paula? She went out to get toilet paper and never came back!" she said anxiously.

Meatboy had forgotten about the toilet paper. Then he remembered the train tramps. "Oh no! I hope she didn't run into those fuckin' assholes!" He threw open the door and looked anxiously up and down the back alley. Silvi stepped out behind him.

"What assholes?"

"Those turkeys we scrapped with at the train yard were here earlier. Didn't you see them?"

"I was upstairs most of the night," Silvi admitted.

"Shit!" swore Meatboy picking up a plastic shopping bag from the ground. He reached in and pulled out the receipt. In the light from the door he could read the items purchased: 8 rolls Purex Tissue, 1 package spearmint chewing gum. The toilet paper was nowhere in sight, probably carted off by a passing scavenger. "Fuck!" screamed Meatboy. Some kind of bad shit had gone down here, and it was all his fault.

"Now what, Whitney? Where are we gonna go? What are we gonna do?" Leo asked fearfully. He couldn't believe what was happening. How could Whitney act like such a beast? Nervousness caused him to blow a stop sign and nearly pee in his pants.

"Just shut up for a minute! I gotta think!" thundered Whitney. Jeez that poof could get on his nerves fast. He supposed he should be grateful. After all, Leo had rushed right down to pick him up after the car crash and had carefully attended to his many cuts and scrapes. After Leo had supplied him with two Tylenol 3's and several shots of brandy, they had waited until nightfall before setting off in pursuit of the money. He was already regretting his impulsive decision to hire the drunken bums in the back seat. And the girl in the trunk? What was he thinking? There had to be a way to turn things around. If those idiots in the back seat would just stop fighting over the last of the sherry he might be able to concentrate.

In the trunk Paula twisted in vain to loosen the duct tape that bound her tightly. Another large strip of the sticky tape covered her mouth forcing her to breath through her nose. Dust from the trunk's interior tickled her nose hairs making her want to sneeze. She tried hard not to panic but a large insect crawled over her ankle and she screamed into the tape. In an effort to regain her cool she forced herself to think of her childhood.

Growing up as a tomboy had not been easy. Not only did she have to tolerate constant roughhousing from her older brothers, but she had to watch out for her younger siblings as well. Mom and Dad had done what they could, but because one or both of them was usually at work, parental guidance was minimal at best. Still, this arrangement suited Paula just fine. She had never been comfortable with authority figures and had gravitated towards rabble-rousers and troublemakers at an early age. Slightly dyslexic and short of attention she had struggled through school, hating each day more than the last one. Finally punk had come along and shown her it was okay not to fit in.

But none of this was helping her now. Paula had recognized the tramps who grabbed her, but who the hell were the other two guys? They sure didn't look like the type of people who would associate with lowlifes like that train trash. In a sudden gut-churning instant it occurred to her that this must have something to do with the money Meatboy had found. They were going to be mad when they found out how much he had spent. As she wondered if she was going to be tortured or killed, the car came to a stop.

"Don't argue with me, Leo! Just go give that punk your phone and come right back!" ordered Whitney. His assistant was being less than cooperative, and kept using words like 'kidnapping' and 'extortion'. Why wouldn't he just do as he was told?

"But what if they beat me up or keep me hostage?" fretted Leo.

"They won't. That wouldn't do them any good, not if they want the bitch back."

Leo got reluctantly out of his car, Whitney sliding over to take the wheel. As he walked the last block to the punkers' hangout, Leo ruminated on the course of action he was on. Maybe it would be best just to go to the police and tell them everything before someone got hurt. He didn't care what happened to him, but he just couldn't bring himself to let Whitney down. With a heavy heart he arrived at the warehouse. Loud music was still issuing from the interior, but Leo had the impression it was taped, not live. He knocked only twice and the door flew open. The green-haired punk he had been chasing for so long stood glowering in the doorway.

"Get lost, party's over!" Meatboy prepared to slam the door.

"Wait! I have an important message for you!" quaked Leo fumbling for his telephone.

Meatboy frowned impatiently. "Well? What the hell is it?"

"This is regarding the dark-haired girl with the leather pants. My boss wants to talk to you." Leo extended the phone.

"Paula?" Meatboy grabbed Leo with both hands, hauling him into the warehouse and slamming him against the wall. "Where is she? If she's been hurt, you are so dead!"

"No! No! She's fine!" said Leo, wondering if she was. "My boss just wants his money back! Here, I'll let you talk to him!" nervously Leo punched in Whitney's number. "Whitney? Here's that fellow you wanted to talk to."

Meatboy snatched the phone from Leo's hand. "Where's my girlfriend, you fuckin' asshole!"

"Calm down," said Whitney smoothly. "You can have her back as soon as you return my backpack."

"Who the hell are you anyway? And why did you leave that money in the park?"

"None of that is important to you. What is important is that you bring the backpack to Britannia park in half an hour if you want to see your sweetheart alive," Whitney said, hoping the punk actually gave a shit about the girl.

"Half an hour!" wailed Meatboy. It wasn't much time.

"I know you didn't put that money in a bank. Get it, and meet me at the statue in Britannia Park at two o'clock or the girl is history." And aware that he was sounding like Mickey Spillane, he added, "And come alone."

21

Meatboy pulled on his jacket and checked to make sure he had his car keys.

"What's going on," asked Silvi worriedly. "Is Paula okay?"

"She'd better be!" growled Meatboy on his way out the door. "Tell those guys I'll be back soon."

The Parisienne purred like a kitten but Meatboy was in no mood to appreciate the automobile's mechanical fitness. Stomping on the gas, he sent up a spray of loose gravel as he rocketed from the parking lot. Other than taxis and drunks, few cars were on the road as he sped down Venables St. towards the bus station. Meatboy drove as fast as he dared, trying to escape the black cloud that hung over his head. Screeching to a halt in front of the bus station, he reached under his shirt to unfasten the key from his nipple ring. A couple of juvenile gangbangers eyed him speculatively as he removed the backpack from the locker. An attack on a lone punk was not entirely out of the question.

"Hey man, what's in the bag?"

"Fuck off!" Meatboy snarled with such vehemence that the bangers abruptly backed off. Adrenaline sang in his veins, and for a moment he wished the youths would try him on. In his furious state he would be happy to rip their arms off and beat them with the bloody appendages. Exiting the station, he glanced at a clock on the wall and saw that he only had ten minutes left to make it back to the park. It was just as well the bangers had backed down; he didn't have time to fight. Jumping into the Parisienne, he put the accelerator to the floorboard and zoomed back up Venables at a hundred miles an hour. He assumed that the money had to be part of some dope deal gone sour, and it occurred to him that the owner was not going to be happy when he found out how much of it was missing. Reaching over, he undid the buckles and removed two bundles. What difference would another twenty thousand make? Now the pack was little more than half full. It was amazing how fast money went when you didn't really care what you spent it on.

Shoving the cash under the seat, he drove towards the park and tried to figure out how he was going to handle this. To his shock, he realised that the money was of no real concern to him, and definitely wasn't worth getting anyone killed over. Stupid money. Why did it have to be so useful?

Meatboy parked the convertible on a side street, grabbed the backpack and covered the last half block to the park on foot.

Leo sat miserably at the base of the statue, his head in his hands. At the sound of Meatboy's approaching footsteps, he looked up anxiously.

"Here's the money. Now where's Paula!" Meatboy demanded, throwing the backpack down at Leo's feet.

Leo stood up and seized the money. "She'll be released two blocks away, in ten minutes." He prepared to depart.

"No fuckin' way!" snarled Meatboy grabbing the bag from Leo's hands. "I wanna see her right now!"

Despite the cool night air, sweat gleamed on Leo's brow. He hadn't been prepared for this—kidnapping was not his field of expertise. "Let me call Whi—my boss." He reached slowly into his pocket and pulled out his phone.

"Make it fast!" snapped Meatboy.

Leo punched in Whitney's number and waited for a reply. "It's me. The guy says he won't give me the bag until he sees the girl." He listened intently for a moment before hanging up and returning the phone to his pocket. "He says okay. I'll take you to her."

Meatboy and Leo crossed the park and walked west on Charles St. As they approached the end of the block, they could see a group of men leaning against the side of a beige, five-year old Ford. Under the glare of the street light, Meatboy recognized the surly faces of the train tramps. With them was a well dressed suit. Dried bits of blood and several bruises marred his otherwise smooth, aristocratic features.

"What the fuck are you guys doing here?" Meatboy glowered at the tramps.

"None a yer fuckin' business!" answered Earl hotly. This would be a good time to give that green-haired freak a few more bruises for his collection.

"Gentlemen!" said Whitney holding up his hands diplomatically. "I believe we have more important business to attend to than your petty squabbles." He moved to the back of the car and popped open the trunk lid. Paula glared up at them furiously. Meatboy thrust the backpack at Whitney, and with a quick motion, ripped the strip of tape from Paula's mouth.

"Yowch!" howled Paula. "How dare you bastards stick me in the trunk like an old carpet!"

"Shhh!" Meatboy admonished. "Let's get out of here!" He leaned into the trunk and began struggling with the tape around Paula's ankles.

"Fuck quiet!" shouted Paula. "I want these assholes fed to the tigers!" She was livid.

Meatboy finally succeeded in freeing the enraged woman. Paula jumped out of the trunk, and in one smooth motion kicked Otis square in the gut. The tramp doubled over and puked explosively, sherry hitting pavement with a foul splash. Whitney ran around the front of the car and prepared to climb into the driver's seat, completely ignoring Leo who stood speechless on the sidewalk. As he transferred the backpack to his left hand to open the door, Bad Eddie snatched the bag from Whitney's hand and dashed towards a narrow back lane. Whitney flipped out. He hadn't come this far to have the money grabbed by some drunken train tramp. Unsnapping his .38 from the ankle holster, he fired off three shots at the fleeing hobo. Bad Eddie staggered and dropped the pack but continued his flight. Stopping was not an option.

Meatboy drove an elbow into Whitney's temple. The stunned politician dropped like a stone, his gun clattering across the asphalt and under a parked car.

"Let's split!" yelled Meatboy grabbing Paula by the arm and hauling her roughly away. The pair dashed down the back lane, Meatboy pausing to snatch up the backpack. Bad Eddie was nowhere in sight, but behind them Meatboy heard the ricochet of rapid footsteps. They hustled around the corner to where Meatboy's car was parked. He fumbled for his keys.

"Hurry!" shouted Paula causing Meatboy to drop the keys.

"Shit!" he mumbled.

Otis and Earl came running up just as Meatboy managed to fire up the hot rod.

"C'mere, you bastards!" screamed Otis. Girls were always beating up on him. Now he was angry.

Meatboy dropped the car into first and laid down twin strips of rubber, the frustrated tramps beating harmlessly on the side panels.

"HAW! HAW! HAW!" crowed Meatboy as the car careened down the street, "What a complete and utter bunch of smegheads!"

"I don't know what you're laughing about. Those assholes will be plenty mad, and they know where you live!"

This realization sobered Meatboy, the laughter dying on his lips. He let up on the accelerator. "Shit!" he cursed. "We better get back there and warn them!" He pulled a tight U-turn and, bouncing over a boulevard, headed back towards the warehouse.

"I hope they don't get there before we do," worried Paula.

The sound of police sirens filling his ears, Whitney retrieved his .38 and jumped behind the wheel of Leo's car.

"You shot that guy, Whitney! He could be dying!" whimpered Leo. He was in shock and couldn't believe how coldhearted his boss was. This wasn't the man he thought he knew.

"Just shut the fuck up, Leo! I haven't the patience to listen to your whining." He put the car in reverse and backed out onto the street. The rear doors opened and Otis and Earl piled into the car.

"What the hell do you guys want? I ought to shoot you both right now!" barked Whitney. He was so bowled over by the audacity of the duplicitous tramps he neglected to put the car into drive. They sat idling in the middle of the street.

"We didn't know Eddie was gonna pull that shit, I swear!" said Earl with as much conviction as he could muster. "Don't you think we should be going?"

Unable to decide the fate of the hobos, Whitney slapped the Tempo into drive and sped towards the punks' warehouse.

"What will you do now, Whitney? The cops will be all over the place!" Leo was unable to stop whining; he just couldn't help it.

"Maybe you don't understand," said Whitney making a herculean effort not to explode. "*I have to get that fucking money back!*"

"We'll help you. We owe those guys," volunteered Earl. Now that he knew Whitney was packing, he was eager to extract revenge.

Whitney knew he could use all the help he could get, even if it did come from these unreliable stooges. "Okay," he said. "Just keep the rest of those punkers off my back." He pulled up behind Meatboy's parked car.

Inside the warehouse punks were still drinking beer and trying to get laid. Members of Fire in the Hole were frantically stripping the stage of everything they could carry.

"Maybe those guys won't try coming back in here," Atlas hoped optimistically.

"Well I don't wanna stick around to find out," answered Meatboy. "That suit has a gun!" He made his way to the back door, arms full of microphones and cords. With an elbow he slid back the bolt and kicked open the door. Whitney stood in the threshold, the .38 leveled at his chest.

"Step back into the warehouse," he ordered.

Meatboy dumped the microphones onto the table and yelled as loud as he could. "Hey! Some assholes are trying to rob us! Somebody help me!"

Instantly a large crowd began to form around the intruders at the door. They hesitated when they saw the gun in Whitney's hand, but alcohol and mob bravado kept them from backing off.

Whitney fanned the gun back and forth at the sea of hostile faces. "I don't want to shoot anybody! I just want my money back!" Earl and Otis cowered behind Whitney. Why wasn't the gun scaring the punkers off?

Meatboy broke free from the group and dashed back across the hall to the stage. Seizing the backpack he tore open the top, ripped open the bundles, and began throwing huge handfuls of cash into the air. "You want money! Here's yer fuckin' money!" Grabbing the pack by the bottom, he swung it back and forth, cash flying in every direction. Stunned by the scene, it took the crowd several seconds to react. Then all hell broke loose.

"Nooooo! That's my money!" screamed Whitney. Jamming the gun into his belt, he threw himself headfirst into the wild throng. Otis and Earl, agog at the sight of so much cash, ran about the edges of the fray snatching up whatever loose bills floated their way.

The Rat had his knife out. Anyone messing with his friends was going to get stuck. "What do ya wanna do now?" he shouted.

"Now we get the fuck outta here!" hollered Meatboy. He picked up a Marshall amplifier and dodged the fighting mayhem for the back door. Tommy, restraining himself from jumping into the mob, picked up his bass guitar and used it as a scythe to chop his way through the bedlam. Atlas followed his example using a stage monitor to bulldoze a path. At the back door, Meatboy looked back at the scene of frantic chaos. The entire hall was consumed with screaming, shoving punks battling for dollars. The suit was nowhere to be seen and must have been swallowed up by the crazed fortune grabbers. Paula and Silvi were already in the car.

"Let's go!" urged Silvi.

Squeezing as much gear into the trunk as possible, the band members forced themselves into the car. At the last moment the Rat staggered out the door, his arms full of cymbal stands. Cramming the hardware into the already overloaded trunk, he dived head first through the open back window. Meatboy flicked on his headlights: he was boxed in by Leo's Ford Tempo.

"Hang on!" he shouted. Inching up to the Tempo's bumper, he floored the accelerator and pushed it, smoking into the back lane. Meatboy aimed the car for the street and looked back for Silvi, who was buried under a writhing pile of bodies in the back seat.

"Got room for a couple people over at your place?" he asked innocently.

22

Tommy sat up in bed as if launched by a spring. Seconds earlier he had been in a deep sleep, but without warning his subconscious jolted him awake. Although he couldn't recall what he had been dreaming, he knew suddenly where he had seen Meatboy before.

"Wake up, Silvi! Wake up!"

Silvi stirred groggily in her sleep. "Errgh. Whazzup? Iz Paula okay? Iza house on fire?" Strands of fine, blonde hair clung to her face like corn silk and her green-lidded eyes were heavy with sleep.

"I know where I've seen Meatboy before! I used to hang out with him when I was a kid! His real name is Terry Michaels! He loosened the front wheels of my soapbox racer, that bastard!" Tommy's nerves hummed with intensity.

"What the hell is wrong with you? My best friend got kidnapped, Meatboy threw away his money, your jam space is probably thrashed, and you're worried about some stupid shit what happened when you were kids?" Silvi was not amused.

Tommy was silent for a moment. For some reason his recollection of the childhood prank was more important than any current event. "You don't understand! I was winning! I woulda won!" Tommy jumped out of bed and began stalking around naked. Revenge was best served cold.

"Big deal!" said Silvi shaking her head and sitting up on the edge of the bed. "You were just kids! Look how generous he's been to you lately!" She was wide awake now, the memories of the previous evening flooding back. If this childishness took precedent over what was happening now, he had serious issues.

Tommy paused again. It was true Meatboy had more than made up for the prank. The more he thought about it, the sillier his anger seemed. Still, he had promised himself that he would get even and he was not one to forget debts owed. There had to be some way to show Meatboy he had not forgotten.

In the kitchen, Meatboy's one good eye popped open. He could see Atlas rooting through the fridge from his perspective on the floor. The big ape had a jar of mayonnaise in one hand, a loaf of bread in the other. Kicking the fridge door closed, he stepped over Meatboy and deposited his prizes on the counter. Enthusiastically he set about building himself a sandwich.

"Fer fucks sakes!" grumbled Meatboy. "Don't you ever stop eating?"

"Not unless I have to," replied Atlas slicing a tomato.

Meatboy slowly climbed to his feet using the kitchen table for support. His stomach lurched as he remembered the kidnapping and loss of money. For a sickening moment, he wasn't sure if she was safe. His memory had gaping holes in it. "Where's Paula?" he asked in a near panic.

"She went home. Said for you to call her when you woke up." Atlas finished construction and took an enormous bite of his sandwich.

Meatboy checked the refrigerator. Fortunately two beer still remained. Popping a tab, he set off in search of the telephone. In the living room, the Rat snored comfortably from his usual spot on the carpet. The enigmatic drummer seemed to prefer floors over couches, probably from habit. Locating the phone under Tommy's leather jacket, Meatboy punched in Paula's number. She answered on the fourth ring.

"Hullo?" She was still half asleep.

"Hi." Just hearing her voice set him at ease.

"Oh hi, Meatboy. Sorry for taking off, but since you were passed out on the floor I didn't think you'd mind." Although she hadn't changed her mind about sleeping with him, she was beginning to think of him as her boyfriend. Damn him!

"You okay?" Meatboy asked solicitously. "Ya wanna go out for Dim Sum?"

Paula didn't really want to go out but Meatboy was so bloody persistent. "I guess we could do that," she agreed reluctantly. "You gonna come get me?"

Meatboy hid his surprise. He didn't think she would accept his offer so readily. "Sure, I'll be right over. See ya inna bit." He hung up the phone and took a big hit of beer. Atlas strolled into the living room, his hand buried in a family-sized box of generic corn flakes.

"Goin' ta see Paula?"

"Yeah, I think I'll go see if she's okay." He pulled on his jacket and emptied his beer with one long, sustained guzzle.

"Did you guys have sex yet?" asked Atlas with his mouth full.

Meatboy glared at him, but saw the hungry guitarist was just curious, not maliciously poking fun at his efforts. "I'm workin' on it, big guy," he grinned. "Tell the boys I'll be back later and we'll go see if our jam space is still standing."

In the light of day, Meatboy saw that his car was the worse for wear from last night's activities. Beer cans and cigarette ashes littered the back seat and a black underwire bra hung from a door handle. Uncharacteristically allowing the engine to warm for several seconds, Meatboy thought back. He didn't remember seeing any tits. Oh well, he thought, backing out onto the street, maybe he would get to see Paula's later. Nailing the gas, he thrilled as the G-forces pressed him back in his seat. Man he loved this car.

Paula was waiting for him outside her apartment building when he arrived. Despite last night's imbroglio, she looked especially tantalizing. Her spiky hair framed her sassy face and her leather skirt clung to her butt like a teenage wet dream. She climbed into the front seat, skirt riding high on silky thighs. Tilting the rearview mirror, she put the finishing touches on her make-up.

"Don't you ever sleep in?" she asked brusquely. "I thought you'd be tired after all that.

Meatboy smirked. "I guess I can afford to sleep now. I won't have all that pesky money keeping me awake," he said with a sardonic grin.

"I know I didn't thank you for last night, but you have to admit those idiots wouldn't have grabbed me in the first place if it wasn't for you." Still, Paula acknowledged, he had given up the money unflinchingly for her, and she probably owed him more of a thank you than that. Maybe later. As far as she was concerned, it was just as well the money was gone. Now things could return to normal. Whatever that was.

"Do you have any cash left?" She was afraid that if he was completely tapped he would hold her responsible. Who would pay for the Dim Sum?

Meatboy powered around a corner. "Reach under your seat."

Feeling around through the loose beer cans, Paula's fingers closed around a stack of paper. Pulling it out, she saw it was a bundle of hundred dollar bills.

"You held out on those guys?" she asked feeling less special. The idea of Meatboy sacrificing all his money was much more romantic. It was strange, thought Paula, although she routinely pushed men away and thought flowers were for sissies, she still felt a fairy-book romance would eventually fall her way. She cursed herself for being so sickeningly normal.

"There should be another one of those under there somewhere, too," said Meatboy making a hard right down a familiar alley. Paula looked up with alarm. They were returning to the warehouse.

"I thought we were going for Dim Sum!"

"We are, but I figured we could just stop by and see what the place looks like," reasoned Meatboy pulling up behind the loading dock.

Paula sat quietly. She wasn't wild about being any-where near this place. Meatboy got out of the car and cautiously approached the building. A single sheet of white paper was taped to the door. Frowning, he tore down the eviction notice and crumpled it into a ball. Paula watched as he opened the unlocked door and stepped inside.

"Hey, Paula. Come in here, the coast is clear!"

With trepidation, Paula joined Meatboy inside. The hall smelled like a beer can full of cigarette butts.

"Amazing!" exclaimed Meatboy, "Our P.A. is still here!" If it hadn't been for the possibility of getting shot, he never would have abandoned the sound system in the first place. He felt like a coward for throwing the money away, but being rich had proved to be more stressful than it was worth. Let those idiots rip each other to shreds over it. Looking around at the decimated building, he wished only that he had videotaped the event for future chuckles.

The stage and all the speaker cabinets still stood intact, but the rest of the hall had not fared so well. It looked like the Battle of Batoche had been waged on-site. Tables and chairs reduced to kindling, broken bottles, and smashed glass lay strewn from one end of the hall to the other. Closer inspection revealed splatters of blood, shredded clothing, assorted punk gear, and other ragged evidence of a prolonged, hard fought engagement. Not a trace of money remained.

"Holy shit!" choked Paula, "We're lucky the Crime Scene Unit isn't here!" She was glad she didn't have to clean it up.

Meatboy continued to survey the wreckage, not knowing what he was looking for—punk gear, money, limbs, musical equipment, Jimmy Hoffa. "Good thing I didn't rent this place under my real name!" he said with relief. "We better get the rest of our shit outta here fast!" He climbed up on the stage and brushed broken glass from Tommy's bass speaker cabinet.

"Don't worry, you've got fourteen days to move out after an eviction for noise, and if you want you can take it to arbitration." Bending over, she picked a scrap of clothing from the floor. "Check this out!" Meatboy looked closer. It was the sleeve of a pin-striped suit jacket.

"Oh, man," groaned Meatboy. "I don't even wanna know what happened to that asshole. Let's get the fuck outta here!"

Paula couldn't have agreed more. The pair got back into Meatboy's car and left the area as quietly as his Thrush mufflers would allow.

It was hard to keep his car on the road with a spinning head. Meatboy was confused — the remaining twenty thousand dollars were fast becoming twenty thousand problems. A simple solution took form in his head. "I'm gonna blow the rest of this cash in style!" he said running a red light. "Are you with me?"

Paula knew she had to see this. What could he possibly do for an encore? "Maybe we should get some beer first?" she answered dazedly.

Meatboy drove down Commercial Drive and took a left on Hastings. Impulsively ignoring a beer store, he looked out the window at the skinny, malnourished wretches walking by. They could use another good meal other than the mandatory Christmas handout at the church. He pulled over and parked outside Save-On-Meats.

Stepping out of the car, he sauntered around to the passenger side and opened Paula's door with mock gentility. She stared up at him.

"What exactly do you have in mind?"

"You'll see," he said mysteriously. "Let's go."

Paula followed Meatboy into the butcher. As usual, the place was doing brisk business. A white-aproned clerk came to take his order.

"Can I help you?"

Meatboy put a handful of hundred dollar bills on the counter. "Yeah," he said. "I want steaks, good ones. T-bones, sirloins, whatever ya got. All of em."

The clerk looked at the pile of cash. "Yes sir!" He turned and spoke briefly with another clerk. Both employees quickly began filling sturdy waxed boxes with thick slabs of red meat. Meatboy stepped outside for a smoke.

Stunned, Paula followed him out onto the street. "What the fuck you up to? Whaddya gonna do with all those steaks?"

Meatboy fired up his cigarette. "I'm gonna give 'em to the soup kitchen on Alexander St," he said decisively. They had been good to him once.

"What about the vegetarians?" asked Paula mockingly. "Not everybody eats red meat!"

"Fuck 'em! Ya ever hear anybody callin' me Broccoli Boy?"

23

Tied naked to his chair, Whitney watched helplessly as the bald seven foot giant approached, a curved, wicked-looking dagger in his hand.

"No! I didn't do it! I'm sorry!" he screeched.

The giant ignored the terrified politician's pitiful entreaties. Slowly, he inserted the tip of the knife into Whitney's eye and began to slice vertically.

It was time for budget cuts.

"AAAAGGGHHH!" shouted Whitney sitting bolt upright. His body was sheathed in sweat and his heart beat wildly. Looking around in panic, he took in the unfamiliar surroundings and realised he had no idea where he was. Then the disastrous evening started filtering back. Oh shit, he thought with a shudder.

Leo reached over from his chair by the bedside and mopped Whitney's feverish forehead with a cool, damp rag. "I'm so glad you're awake! I was so worried!"

Whitney noticed that his demolished suit jacket and irreparably scuffed shoes had been removed. With relief he saw he was still wearing the rest of his ripped, stained clothing. The idea of Leo undressing him sent violent little bumps rippling up and down his spine. Rubbing his puffy eyes, he swung his legs over the edge of the lumpy mattress and waited for a bolt of lightning to strike him. What a fucking mess.

"Where the hell are we, and how did we get here?" He saw Leo's face was haggard from lack of sleep. The idiot looked like he had been up fretting and fussing all night.

"We're at the Waldorf Hotel on Hastings. I managed to drag you away from that warehouse. You must have been delirious, those punks were trying to kill you!"

"What happened to the money?" asked Whitney, expecting the worst.

"You managed to get some of it, but I'm afraid those punkers got the lion's share. There was nothing I could do!"

"How much did I get? Where is it?" he asked feeling a wave of nausea rise up in his stomach. He fought it down with a hard swallow.

"I uncrumpled and counted it. You had money stuffed in every pocket, down your pants, in your shirt—it was everywhere!"

"You took it out of my pants?" The puke tsunami threatened to return. "How much money do I have?" he repeated, not really wanting to know.

Leo hesitated. Whitney was not going to be happy. "Not counting small pieces, you have fifty-seven hundred dollars. A lot of the bills were ripped or torn in half."

"Fifty-seven hundred!" moaned Whitney. "I'm screwed!" Thank god it was Saturday, at least nobody at the office would be looking for him. He knew he could stall Braden no longer, and now he couldn't even return the money. If he cleaned out his bank account he might be able to flee the country, Brazil perhaps, at least until he had enough time to figure things out. He had only one option. Bail. Split. Vamoose.

"Listen carefully, Leo. I'm going to leave town for a while. Give me a lift to my house so I can pick up a few things, then I need a ride to the airport." It seemed like a drastic measure, but there was no way around it.

"I'm so sorry all this happened, Whitney. I wish there was something I could do!" Leo handed him a bulky envelope full of mangled money.

"Yeah, whatever. Let's go."

Leo had anticipated such a maneuver and had already paid for the room and packed. Since he had used up a week of his vacation time on the undercover mission, Whitney owed him personally. However, he was afraid to broach the subject and hoped hollowly that Whitney would offer the payment. Knowing the Minister as he did, he figured this was about as likely as it was for Bill Clinton to be forthcoming about his sex life. As much as he hated to admit it, things probably weren't going to work out between him and Whitney.

Out on the sidewalk, the conniving Minister had another surprise in store for his faithful employee.

"Give me the keys," he demanded. "I'll drive."

While Leo didn't understand why Whitney wanted to drive, he did as instructed. He had already argued strenuously over the matter of the kidnapping and didn't want to aggravate his boss further. Taking the keys, Whitney got in the driver's seat and reached over to lock the passenger door from the inside.

"Sorry, Leo," he called through the closed window. "You're fired." With no further tasks for Leo to pursue and with his world falling apart, Whitney had no use for an assistant. He pulled into traffic, leaving a dismayed and bewildered man standing abandoned on the sidewalk with some luggage.

In his desire to beat a hasty exit, Whitney turned left instead of right and realised he was going to have to go down Commercial Drive instead of taking the more direct route home. As he proceeded down the street, he noticed that some sort of neighbourhood celebration seemed to be in progress. Groups of people stood laughing and drinking on corners and a festive, party mood hung in the air. As he stopped for a jay-walker, a beer can bounced off the roof of the car. What the hell was going on? Was it welfare day? Just another soccer piss-up? Bursts of music and peals of drunken mirth rang loudly in his ears. The whole street was alive with merriment and gaiety. With a sudden shock, he knew why they were all partying—the fucking bastards were spending the money they had picked from the floor of the warehouse last night. His money! They were laughing at him!

He applied pressure on the gas pedal, nearly creaming two plump young girls staggering across the street. Another denizen, witnessing the near collision, swore loudly and hurled an empty bottle of expensive French wine at Whitney's vehicle. If the police were keeping the peace, they must be doing it somewhere down east, he thought bitterly. Not a single cruiser car was in sight. He turned onto Broadway and tried to block the image of the freeloading bums from his mind.

Trying to decide which of his most valuable possessions to take with him, he parked Leo's car on the street and stepped gratefully to his door. The prospect of leaving all his precious objets d'art behind bothered him almost as much as the thought of being fitted for concrete shoes. He had become attached to his collection of brightly shaped glass and twisty chrome things. Unlocking the door he stepped into the foyer and flicked on the lights. A black figure stepped forward and pressed cold metal against his neck. Unlike his other nightmare, this one was short and had a gun instead of a knife. A face Whitney did not want to see emerged from the depths of his spacious lobby.

"It's about goddamned time!" snarled Braden. "I was almost asleep. Where the hell've ya been? I've been looking for you!"

"Braden!" bluffed Whitney, "I was just about to give you a call!"

"I believe the time for talking is over," said the gangster.

Bad Eddie limped slowly through the heavy underbrush. He knew he was seriously injured and needed hospitalization. Unfortunately he had outstanding warrants and would be arrested if he showed up at an emergency ward. Unable to think clearly through the blinding fog of pain, he did what he knew best. He fled. Steering well clear of the hobo jungle, he picked his way to the cover of an old railway abutment and waited for a ticket out of town.

Presently a large freighter chugged into the yard, its three locomotives hissing softly. Cursing in pain, Bad Eddie hobbled over to wait for an opportunity to hop aboard. At first the train slowed, then began to pick up speed and the injured tramp worried that he might not be able to book passage. Just when he was about to give up, he spotted a rusty cattle car with an open door. Running alongside, Bad Eddie struggled to reach sufficient boarding speed. His aching wounds made all movement extremely painful, but ignoring indignant shrieks of outrage from his tortured nerve endings, he pushed his bullet-ridden body for all it was worth. Reaching maximum possible speed, he felt the moment of truth arrive; it was now or never. Train hopping, like air travel, was most dangerous on takeoffs and landings. One slight miscalculation made for messy results. Grasping the ladder, he attempted to swing himself aboard. With a sharp cry of alarm, his weakened fingers slipped from the ladder rung and Bad Eddie dropped heavily onto the tracks. Rolling instinctively away from the enormous steel beast, he prayed he had been quick enough to avoid being crushed. With a start of pure terror, he felt the cold steel of the railway track beneath his neck. A massive wheel bore down on him. Shit! he thought. I'm dea—

24

Contrary to scientific belief, word of free beer travels faster than the speed of light. News of the huge block party had spread throughout the city and freeloaders everywhere were either on the scene or on the way. Nobody wanted to take a chance that rumours of hundred dollar bills being handed out might be false. Depending on how you viewed large, noisy congregations and the mass consumption of alcohol, this was either a righteous street party or a serious law enforcement problem. Commercial Drive was party cake and everyone wanted a slice.

The party, merely a continuation of the previous evening, was now reaching epic proportions. Those who had been present for Meatboy's largess were generously offering to share the wealth with those who had missed out. Street dealers and pot merchants had also crawled out of the woodwork and were setting record sales. Everyone was talking about the money, but by now vastly different versions as to where it came from were so ridiculous as to be unbelievable. One tale had a man dressed as Santa Claus handing out bundles of cash on the street; another, an ATM spitting out money. The only thing everyone agreed on was that someone had sure spread out the greenbacks.

Shopkeepers gloated lubriciously. All the restaurants, bars and coffee shops were jammed to capacity with even more people spilling onto the streets and crowding the parks. Jugglers, buskers and fire-eaters were out in full force and making a fortune. Other than a natural amount of breakage and spillage, the party was proceeding peacefully and the air was full of pot smoke and laughter. The sun broke through the clouds and cast feeble rays of sunshine down on the rejoicing subjects. Even the usually constant wail of sirens and ambulances was noticeably absent.

In the last three hours Meatboy and Paula had done a good job of providing the East Vancouver food banks and soup kitchens with a higher grade of food than they had ever seen. Paula had argued that it would have been more helpful if he had bought less expensive cuts of meats and cheaper vegetables, but Meatboy was not to be swayed from his vision. "Why feed 'em all the same crap they get everyday?" he reasoned. "They need something to brighten things up a bit, and nothing cheers you up like a good T-bone steak!"

"Try telling that to a vegan," Paula had rejoined.

Now with less than three thousand dollars left to his name—which he planned to save for another practice space—he and Paula had returned to Commercial Drive to join the party they had created. A sense of fulfillment pinged at his soul.

As the streets were clogged with merrymakers, Meatboy and Paula had only been able to get as far as Silvi's before they were forced to park the Parisienne and proceed on foot. "You'd think some of these people would save money for their college educations," Meatboy quipped sarcastically. He took a hit of beer and watched a pissed young punk shinny up a light standard.

"So how about telling me what that was all about now?" asked Paula giving Meatboy a quizzical look.

"What was what all about?" he replied innocently.

"Don't give me that bullshit! You know exactly what I'm talking about! Why this nice guy act all of a sudden?"

Meatboy did his best to look offended. "I'm just trying to give people a break. It didn't cost me nothing!" In reality, he wasn't sure what had gotten into him. He had a feeling he was going to regret his generosity later, and was giddy from spending so much money so fast. Paula wasn't at all satisfied with his answer but sensed she would gain nothing further from her companion. She pulled a beer from her jacket and gave Meatboy a final suspicious look. This wasn't over yet.

Familiar faces began to appear in the crowd and soon Meatboy found himself surrounded by fans and admirers.

"That was the dopest show I ever seen!" claimed one young fan.

"Do ya have any records or CD's?" asked another.

"We should have a single out by next week," Meatboy assured them importantly.

Ignored by the horde of drunk supporters, Paula stood back and studied Meatboy with amusement. He didn't seem completely at ease with his new found popularity but as usual was trying to bluster his way through it. Given time, she figured, he would let this stuff go to his head. But then again, part of her felt he deserved the praise, and this possibility made her ashamed of her negative thoughts. What was it with this guy? She never had any trouble deciding who she had wanted to date before, so why did her feelings for Meatboy keep changing? Was some of his bullshit rubbing off on her?

"C'mon, let's go see if we can find the rest of the band," she suggested, tugging Meatboy's sleeve. "They must be around here somewhere."

The local celebrity reluctantly dragged himself away from his fans. Drinking beer and chatting with well-wishers, Paula and Meatboy drifted slowly down the street keeping a casual eye out for other members of the band. It had been a long day and soon Paula began to tire of being jostled on the crowded sidewalks.

"They're probably over at Silvi's, sleeping," she hinted wistfully. She could use a nap herself.

"Let's go over to the park for a bit. If we can't find them, we'll go over to Silvi's," said Meatboy, still not convinced his fans didn't need him.

Paula was too tired to argue. Turning down a side street, they twisted their way towards the park. Meatboy cautiously put his arm around Paula and found, to his surprise, she didn't resist. When he felt a sharp object poke him in the kidney, he first thought it was Paula's rebuff. A voice growled in his ear. "Keep walking till we get to the alley."

Shocked out of his happy complacency, he turned his head to see Earl and Otis tightly flanking him, sharp knives held low at their sides.

"Aw, fer chrissakes! Don't you guy's ever quit?" He was in too good a mood to have things fouled up by these clowns.

"Shut up, and turn down this alley," Earl ordered.

Paula attempted to make a run for it but Otis had her firmly by the upper arm. "Ow! Lemme go, you fuckin' creep!" She glared furiously at her assailants.

"What the hell do you guys want, anyway?" asked Meatboy. "You saw me throw the money away last night! It's all gone!"

"We don't believe it. You wouldn't be stupid enough to throw away all of that money," said Earl meaningfully. "So cough it up."

Meatboy remembered he did have some of the money left, but damned if he was gonna give it to these morons. "Listen, if you didn't get your share last night, that's your tough luck. Now why don't you guys just take a walk and we'll pretend this never happened."

Paula chose that moment to reverse Otis' grip, twisting his arm behind his back and causing him to drop his knife. The judo lessons she had received from her older brothers had not been wasted.

"Aaaahhhh!" screeched the disabled train tramp. His earlier shoulder injury sent searing rockets of agony into his brain. Meatboy used this diversion to slam his half-full can of beer into Earl's head with all the force he could muster. The aluminum crumpled flat, sending beer foam spurting through the air. Instinctively Earl drove his knife forward, dirty stainless steel sliding through leather into flesh. A shocked look appeared on Meatboy's face as he staggered backwards clutching his side. With a violent spin, Otis wrenched himself free and lunged at Paula. She sidestepped the hobo and planted a steel cap in his shin, causing him to yelp even louder. Dodging the incapacitated hobo she ran out onto the street, hollering at the top of her lungs. "Hey! Listen up everybody! The guy who gave you all the money just got stabbed by two creeps over here!" She waved her arms and pointed at Otis and Earl who had quit the alley and were attempting to slip away. Several people, afraid to get involved, pretended they hadn't heard and kept walking. Others stopped, unsure how to react. Paula yelled again.

"Help me, you bastards! They're getting away!" Again she pointed at the fleeing tramps. An unkempt man with long, dirty blonde hair reached out and seized Otis by the collar. His action prompted others to jump in, and within seconds Otis and Earl were completely surrounded by an angry mob. A large, tattooed young woman with beefy arms and a crewcut grabbed Earl by his stringy hair.

"Is this one of 'em, honey?" she said, giving Earl a vicious shake.

Paula broke through the mob and began raining furious, solid blows down on the struggling train tramp's head. "You fucking bastard! You stabbed my boyfriend!"

Earl tried to protect his face from the punishing fists. "Lemme go! I never seen this broad before! She's nuts!"

Now Otis was completely besieged. Four punk rockers had him in a crossfire and were beating the bloody bejesus out of him. In an effort to minimize the damage, he curled into a fetal ball and instinctively clasped his head in his hands. The mob, bloodlust rising, lashed out at the unfortunate hobos with rabid intensity. So bent on destruction were they that they failed to notice the person whom they were ostensibly saving lurch from the alley, his hands covered with gore.

"Let 'em go," Meatboy croaked. "Don't let 'em ruin our party. They ain't worth it!" Slumping against a wall, he slid to the ground leaving a dark smear of blood. Diverted from the lynching, the mob took a collective pause. Most of them had no idea who they were beating or why. Several of the clearer heads prevailed and gave Otis and Earl a chance to scramble to their feet. Breaking free from the mob, they fled for their lives. Feeling cheated and sensing there was to be no further retribution, the crowd rained bricks and empty bottles down on the fleeing tramps.

Paula rushed over to Meatboy. Pulling back his leather jacket she saw the neat slit in his WE'RE THE

MEATMEN AND YOU SUCK T-shirt. Already the blood had stained the shirt crimson and was spreading in an ever-widening circle. Meatboy looked up at her, his face pale.

"I think I better lie down for a bit. I don't feel so hot," he mumbled. His eyes closed halfway and he tipped slowly onto the grass.

Paula leaned over anxiously to check Meatboy's pulse. A bright red bubble formed on his lips; she thought he was doing a remarkable job of imitating somebody about to die. An airliner droned lazily overhead.

"Holy shit," said the tattooed young woman. "He's fucked up bad!"

Paula shook her head. She jumped up, yelled. "Somebody phone a fucking ambulance!"

25

The writing on the wall was clear. Otis and Earl had overstayed their welcome in Vancouver and the sooner they departed the better. Nursing new contusions and massaging fresh bruises, the aching train tramps hobbled slowly back to the train yard. Topping the hillock separating the train yard from the street, they were confronted with a myriad of flashing lights and a profusion of rescue vehicles. Emergency personnel clustered around a section of railway track and were slowly shoveling something messy into a bag.

"Shit!" exclaimed Earl. "What the fuck's goin' on down there?"

"It doesn't really matter does it? The train is stopped. We're gonna have to walk farther down the tracks and try our luck elsewhere."

Cursing their bad luck and the younger generation they felt was responsible for the delay, the tramps retraced their steps and trudged painfully onwards. Otis was beginning to get persnickety. "You better hope that punker isn't dead. All those witnesses, the trial will last about ten minutes."

"Don't be talking no shit. Ya think any of those bums will friendly up to the pigs? Besides it was an accident, that punk fell on my knife! We never would have got into that situation if you hadn't lost all the money we found at the hall!" Earl was in no mood for any crap either.

"How was I supposed ta know my jacket pocket had a hole in it? Why didn't you hang on to the money?"

And so it went. Recrimination followed recrimination until eventually they were merely repeating themselves. Finally they found a suitable spot to wait for a ride out of town. A heavy, bitter silence hung between them. Earl spoke first.

"Otis. I hate you."

His partner sulked even harder. Reaching into a pocket of his jacket that wasn't ripped, he fished out a half-empty bottle of rice wine. "Guess you won't be needing any of this, then."

In the distance, a train whistle signaled the arrival of their carriage.

Tommy chuckled to himself as he unlocked the trunk of Meatboy's car and threw the lug wrench inside. It had taken him a long time to figure out a suitable plan of revenge, but finally he had stumbled on the answer. Silvi did not share his enthusiasm for the prank and stood glowering on the curb.

"Somebody could get seriously injured, ya know. It's not funny at all!" she folded her arms on her chest and glared at him with a look that guaranteed him he wouldn't be getting any soon.

"Aw, relax! He won't get a chance to go fast enough that he'd hurt himself! This is important, I have a score to settle!" While it bothered him that Silvi couldn't see the necessity of what he was doing, it wasn't about to deter him from his chance for payback. Wiping his greasy hands on his jeans, he did a double take when he saw Paula running towards them.

"Paula! What's going on? Where's Meatboy?"

"No time to explain!" she huffed breathlessly. "In the hospital! Gotta go." She snatched the keys from Tommy with bloody fingers. She jumped into the front seat, started the engine and slammed the car into gear.

"Wait! Paula! You can't take th——"

It was too late. Paula popped the clutch and tromped the gas. With a squeal, the souped-up Parisienne shot away from the curb and barreled down the street. Tommy jumped up and down flailing his arms, watching in horror as the car reached the corner. As Paula attempted to negotiate the curve, the left front wheel separated itself from the car, plowed through a fence, and bounced off a tree. Out of control, the Parisienne careened onto the boulevard and tore deep furrows across a neighbour's front lawn on a collision course with the house. Spitting chunks of sod, the car skidded to a stop two feet away from the front steps. Paula stared straight ahead out the windshield, a stunned expression on her face. The engine stalled.

Tommy ran over to the car, his legs on fire. "Paula! Paula! Are you okay?" He yanked open the door and hauled her limp form out onto the lawn. Snapping out of shock, Paula grabbed Tommy by the front of his T-shirt.

"I gotta get to the hospital!" She was unaware that Tommy's tampering had caused her accident. Indeed, she didn't even seem to care about the crash.

"What's wrong with Meatboy?" asked Tommy. He was relieved that Paula did not appear to be injured, but obviously there were other, bigger problems.

Silvi hugged Paula; she failed to respond and seemed to be in a trance. "Are you okay? Why is Meatboy in the hospital?"

Instead of replying, Paula turned and began trotting down Woodland Drive towards Broadway. Tommy and Silvi rushed to keep up and eventually Paula managed to hail a passing cab. The driver looked uncertain about his wild-looking fares—especially the girl smeared with blood—but drove them directly to their destination as quickly as the law would allow. Throwing a ten dollar bill at the driver, Paula stormed into the emergency ward of the Vancouver General Hospital and rushed over to the information window.

"Which room is Mea—" she turned to Tommy for help. Meatboy's real name had never been important before.

"Terry Michaels," volunteered Tommy.

The nurse on duty peered suspiciously at the trio through her bifocals and consulted the admissions list. "Just a minute, let me see...oh, that must be the young fellow they just brought in. I'm afraid you can't see him right this moment. He's about to go into surgery, he's listed in critical condition."

"I'll wait," said Paula blankly. Turning, she walked over to a row of burnt-orange vinyl couches and joined the ranks of worried-looking strangers waiting for word of their loved ones. Tommy and Silvi followed her over and sat down. With much effort, they finally coaxed the details out of Paula.

"Meatboy let those assholes go?" Tommy asked incredulously. He wanted to find the tramps and turn them into dog food. If only they had never ran into those hobos. If only Atlas had of been a little rougher with them. At least Paula didn't seem bothered about the car wreck or who might be responsible for it. She sat erect and still in her chair, eyes focused on some tiny, unseen object.

Sensing that nothing she could say would comfort her companion, Silvi fumbled in her pockets with shaky hands.

"I gotta go out for a smoke. Wanna join me, Tommy?"

Tommy glanced worriedly at Paula. She was a punk rock statue. "We're going out for a smoke, Paula, be right back." Putting an arm around Silvi's shoulders, he escorted her from the building.

Dried blood flaked from Paula's skin, leaving tiny dark specks on the emergency room floor. Time ticked slowly by.

Atlas and the Rat, entourage in tow, caroused merrily down the street towards Silvi's with the beer. The party on Commercial Drive was still going strong, but the group had elected to try and hook up with their other bandmates. They had been in an apartment overlooking the Drive and had not been able to spot Meatboy or Paula among the revelers. By process of elimination, they had concluded that the singer and his non-girlfriend were probably at Silvi's. The boys were enjoying their new-found celebrity and were basking in the glow of success. Even Atlas had forgotten not to drink and had a fair buzz happening. Seeing a police car and a tow truck at the end of the street, he tapped the Rat on the shoulder.

"Whaz goin' on down there?" he asked curiously.

The Rat had his arm around a young Surrey punkette and hadn't even noticed the emergency vehicles. Squinting down the street, he recognized a familiar car. "Hey! That looks like Meatboy's ride! What happened?"

As they got closer, they could see that it was indeed Meatboy's car. Front end in the air, the auto was hooked up to the back of the tow truck, clods of mud and grass clinging to the brake drum. A tow truck driver was rolling the missing front wheel from a neighbor's yard towards his truck. By now the punks had all noticed the police car and began jettisoning open cans of beer as they approached the scene.

"What's goin' on?" asked the girl on the Rat's arm. She was a short, pretty girl with milky cheeks and big white teeth. A pet rat in her jacket pocket peered out at the world with beady, rodent eyes.

"I dunno," muttered the Rat. "But I'm gonna find out."

Stopping in front of the police car, he addressed a policewoman making notes. "Excuse me, ossifer. What happened here?"

The cop stopped writing and assessed the group with snarly disposition. "Why? You know who owns this vehicle?"

The Rat hated it when cops answered questions with other questions. He shook his head in the negative. "No, but my friend lives in that apartment building and we were just curious."

The cop frowned suspiciously at the sharp-faced young man. "Well, you tell your friend he can pick his car up at the police impound lot. You got any I.D.?"

The Rat pretended to search his pockets. "Must've left it at home."

Taking down the Rat's fictitious name, the cop dismissed the group with a final scowl. The tow truck driver spoke briefly with the cop before getting into his truck and leaving the scene. Hoping to find out about Meatboy's wheelless car, the Rat rang Silvi's buzzer. After the fourth ring, the feeling of apprehension in his stomach began to grow.

"Doesn't look like anybody's home," said Michelle the Surrey punkette.

"Very good, Michelle," responded her friend Nikki. "I bet you did real well in school."

"Shut-up, Nikki! You ain't no rocket scientist neither!"

"Girls, girls," mediated the Rat. "Let's take it outside." Holding the door open for the drunk girls, they left the building. Outside on the street, the group pondered the fate of their companions.

"I wonder what happened to them?" queried Atlas. "I phoned Paula's place earlier, and they're not over there either."

The Rat had a bad feeling about this. "I hope they're okay," he said in a rare display of concern. He cracked open a can of beer and sat down on the curb. As he worried about his mates, a tan BMW pulled up and double-parked in the street. A thin, eager-looking young man wearing a suit jacket and jeans climbed out and approached the group. There was something familiar about the face — the Rat knew him from somewhere.

"I'm looking for Fire in the Hole, aren't you in the group?"

Now the Rat remembered where he had seen this dude. He was the sound engineer from the recording studio. "Yeah, why? Our singles ready?" He wondered how they had turned out. This could be cool.

"That's what I wanted to talk to you about. I liked the song so much I gave it to a DJ I know at the university and he started giving it a lot of airplay. And then the local FM rock station picked it up and gave it some rotation. Next thing I know, DJ's everywhere were calling me, wanting to get copies. The song is taking off like a rocket! Don't you guys ever listen to the radio?"

The group of punkers had stood quietly listening. One of them commented, "Not too often, it's mostly shite."

The Rat remained silent for a moment trying to grasp the significance of the news. "Ya mean they're playing our song on the radio?" This had to be some kind of joke.

"That's what I'm telling you! At least three independent record labels have expressed interest in signing you on. I think if you hold out and have some other good songs, you could get picked up by the majors!" The engineer looked like he was enjoying himself immensely. "Do you guys have a manager? I know a couple people who could probably book you guys on a good tour."

Atlas grinned like a Cheshire cat. "Fuckin' hell! Wait'll Meatboy hears about this!"

26

Meatboy cautiously opened his eyes. Taking in the bile green walls and the stench of disinfectant, he realised he was in a hospital. Damn! He was gonna have to lay off that dummy dust. Then he became aware of an intense pain in his lower abdomen. Now he remembered why he was here. Christ that hurt. It felt like fire ants had chewed a hole through him. Judging by the number of fancy-looking gizmos connected to his body, he must be pretty fucked up. Lifting the sheet he looked down at his stomach, but all he could see was a large, white bandage. On the wall he spotted a button with a sign underneath that read RING FOR ASSISTANCE. He rang. Presently but not shortly, a nurse arrived. Starchy slacks rubbing crisply between chubby thighs, she bustled over and stuck a thermometer in his mouth.

"Welcome back to the land of the living," she said with false bonhomie. "How are we feeling today?" It was automatic, like saying 'Have a nice day'.

Meatboy yanked the thermometer out of his mouth. "Hurtin'. Gimme some drugs, my stomach is killin' me!" He stuck the thermometer back in his mouth and glared expectantly at the nurse.

The nurse clucked disapprovingly over Meatboy's manners. "I'll have the doctor give you some morphine. In the meanwhile, there's a young lady here who would like to see you."

Meatboy's record-player heart skipped. "Paula?"

"I'm not sure what her name is, I'll send her in." Recording her patient's vital signs on a clipboard, she took the thermometer and exited the room.

Paula entered moments later, a frightened look on her face. Seeing all the bells and whistles sticking out of Meatboy, she rushed over and threw her arms about his neck.

"I'm so glad you're okay! I thought you were..."

"Dead?" he finished her sentence. "No such luck. So, I had to get stabbed to get some lovin'? Why didn't you just pretend I got stabbed before?" Smiling, he put his arms around her and breathed in her beery, girl smell.

Paula jerked away from him, fire flashing in her dark eyes. "Just 'cause I was worried about you doesn't mean I care about you!" Caught in a contradiction, she changed the subject. "So, when you gettin' outta here?"

Despite the pain, Meatboy grinned. "I dunno. I gotta talk to the doc. He's supposed to give me some morphine right away. I could use it."

Paula lifted an eyebrow skeptically. "If you were on the street you'd probably just drink a bottle of whisky."

"Maybe, but I'm not on the street, am I?" he said winking at her.

Paula rolled her eyes. Had Meatboy engineered this stabbing just to get drugs? No, she decided, because it was making him miss the party. "Well, that was sure some bash you started. They're probably still at it."

"Why, what time is it? How long have you been here?" Meatboy had no idea how long he had been under, could have been minutes or weeks.

"You came in here about two in the afternoon, it's now three-thirty in the morning."

"Three-thirty! You been waiting here all that time?" Meatboy was aghast. Why would anyone wait that long for him?

Paula blushed. It was the first time he had ever seen her do that. "Well, you know..." she trailed off.

The doctor entered the room looking tired and over-worked. "I'm sorry, I'm going to have to ask you to leave. This patient needs his rest." Producing a hypodermic syringe, he jabbed it into Meatboy's i.v. drip.

"Bye-bye Paula," said Meatboy, eyes closing. "I still want to fuc..."

Paula walked back down the misery-laden hallway to the waiting room. Atlas and the Rat were pacing anxiously.

"Is he gonna be okay?" asked Atlas. He was eating a vending machine apple turnover but deep furrows of concern creased his face.

Paula wasn't sure but there was no point in him being worried. "Yeah, he's gonna be alright. He needs some rest. I'll come back tomorrow and see how he's doing. Let's go get some sleep."

The weary trio stepped out of the hospital and into a waiting taxi. A quick inventory confirmed their fears. They were almost broke.

Meatboy slowly recovered. The knife had pierced his colon and the danger of infection was high. Pumped full of antibiotics and morphine, he had plenty of time to reflect. Should he have given away all the money? Maybe he should have spent it all on liquor, drugs and hookers. He rang the nurse for paper and a pen. Chewing his tongue thoughtfully, he began to write:

216

GRAB A BRAIN

I don't know what it's like to be you,
You don't know what it's like to be me.
But if you looked inside, if you had a brain
You'd see that me and you are just the same.

In another world, in a different life.
Things could have worked out differently.
You could be poor, and I could be rich.
Would you still be the same sonofabitch?

Clothes don't make the man, and money don't mean shit.
Ivy league don't help you none when you're face down in a ditch.
You pass me by on the street, you're afraid, so you look away.
You tell yourself this could never, ever, happen to you someday.

Grab a fucking heart
Grab a fucking brain.
You and me, we're the same inside.
I won't take the blame.

Studying what he had just written, Meatboy realized it was closer to revealing how he actually felt than his usual efforts. Nah, it would never work. Crunching the sheet into a ball, he tossed it into a corner. He began writing a new song, this one about large amounts of alcohol and high-speed police pursuits. He wasn't ready to save the world just yet.

27

"You gonna sign it or not?" Tommy asked impatiently. Meatboy sat at the table, pen in hand, but for some unfathomable reason was stalling. He looked to Paula for advice.

"Don't look at me," she said in the condescending tone of a teacher addressing a young pupil. "You never asked for my help with anything else. Yer gonna have to make this decision all by yourself."

"Sign the dang thing already," urged the Rat. It was as close as he got to swearing. The rest of the band had given the recording contract their John Doe's a long time ago — Meatboy was the last holdout. Gerry, the sound engineer and now manager for Fire in the Hole, raised his eyebrows and waited expectantly. Meatboy finally bent over and scratched his name on the contract.

"There. Y'all happy now?" he picked up the ever-present can of beer from the coffee table and dispatched the contents down his throat. The contract he had just signed obligated the band to produce at least two albums, with the record label handling all distribution and advertising. To maintain full musical direction and integrity, the group had elected to sign with an independent rather than a major label. They had been able to pick and choose for the best deal. This was the stuff dreams were made of. So why did Meatboy feel so deeply dissatisfied? Getting slowly to his feet, he shuffled to the kitchen for another beer.

Gerry voiced his concern to the rest of the band once Meatboy had left the room. "Is he going to be okay to tour? He looks pretty weak." The band was scheduled to fly to Los Angeles next week to kick off their North American tour by opening for Iggy Pop. From L.A. they would share a bus with Kraft Dinner Revenge for thirty-four dates. It was the chance of a lifetime for Fire in the Hole, but it was going to be a lot of work.

"I'll take care of him," promised Atlas. "If he gets tired I'll carry him."

Gerry still looked unconvinced. He had wanted the band to stay in the city to finish recording their first long player, but the band had argued that they didn't even have enough songs for a whole album and that they could write some new tunes on the road. Mostly the boys just wanted to get out and make some noise. Being in a band was a great way to visit places you would not normally be able to afford. Not to mention the booze and the girls.

Meatboy returned from the kitchen, beer in hand. He knew he should be happy, elated even, but he couldn't shake his crushing negativity. "I'm gonna go for a little walk. See you guys in a bit."

Taking the elevator down to the lobby, Meatboy stepped out into the early evening dusk. He liked this time of day, when the city paused between work and play. It was a time to think. Walking slowly, mindful of the hole in his midsection, he made his way to a small park a half block away. Pleased that the park was empty of citizens, he sat down on the only bench and sparked up a smoke. Why wasn't he happy? It wasn't just his inability to score with Paula, and it wasn't the loss of the money. It was something else, and *he didn't know what it was*! His whole life felt like a waste of time; his existence a bad joke. How could he be suffering a mid-life crisis at the tender age of twenty-seven? He was so absorbed in his own inner torment he failed to notice Paula slip onto the bench next to him.

"What's eating you? How come yer not yuckin' it up with the boys?" This was very un-Meatboy-like behavior.

Meatboy was silent. His school teachers had asked him similar questions and he had been either unwilling or unable to give them any answers. Was it the same unnamed problem? Hesitantly he tried to express his frustration. "I dunno, Paula. I know I should be happy, but something's missing. It's like when I'm trying to write a song. I feel like I have something to say but I don't know how to say it. The words are inside somewhere, but they're buried by hesitation or swamped with inhibition.'

'I just wanna shout at people and tell them how stupid we all are, but nobody understands what I'm saying and the people I'm really angry at would never listen to my music anyway. I know I can't change the way people think, but sometimes I wish I could change something! I mean, shit! So I gave away a bunch of money, but that doesn't change nuthin'! The most any of those people will have to show for it tomorrow will be a nasty hangover. When I pick up my pencil and wanna shake the world, all that comes out is stupid songs about drinking beer and fucking. I feel fucking useless, nothing I say matters to anybody. Fuck!" Finishing his rant, he rested his elbows on his knees and put his head in his hands. Oh stupid world.

Paula sat quietly absorbing what Meatboy had said. She was surprised that he had let down his guard. She knew that nobody could be as two-dimensional as he pretended to be, but to see him actually concerned about anything was startling. Up until now she had vainly suspected that his acts of charity had mainly been a clever plot to get her in the sack. Jesus, what if he actually did have a heart?

She put a hand on his shoulder. What could she do? "It's not so much what you say, as how loud you say it. If people don't get your message, send 'em home with bleeding eardrums. Know what I'm saying? Fuck 'em!"

This sentiment struck a responsive chord in Meatboy's heart. Paula was right. Why should he carry the weight of the world when it was more fun just to blow their heads off? Maybe the record label would buy him some louder amplifiers. He lifted his head and smiled. "C'mon, let's go drink some more beer." He finished his beer and tossed the can over his shoulder. Paula stood up and held out her hand.

The band looked up as Meatboy and Paula entered the apartment.

"Hi, guys. What's up?" Atlas asked curiously.

Not responding, Paula led Meatboy into her bedroom and closed the door behind them. Now Meatboy was curious. He hoped this meant what he thought it meant.

Paula gave him a penetrating look. "I know what yer thinking. You're thinking that this is the part where the hero gets to screw the beautiful girl and then goes flying off into the sunset or some crap like that."

"Well, I, er, uh." He didn't know what to think.

Paula stripped off her top and shoved Meatboy onto the bed. "Well yer wrong. You're not fucking anybody. I'm fucking you!" She untied his combat boots and began wrestling them off. Meatboy helpfully unbuckled his jeans and eased them slowly past his knees. He didn't know if he was up to this kind of activity, but he was sure as hell gonna find out. Pushing Meatboy onto his back, Paula peeled off her panties and straddled his face.

"Lick!" she commanded.

°

28

Meatboy wasn't too happy paying four hundred dollars and fifty-two cents to get his car out of the police impound. At least Paula had put the wheel back on and had copped to the 'Leaving the scene of an accident' charge. The police had pointed several sticky questions at her, but she had neatly sidestepped incriminatory statements and managed to sweet talk the impound sergeant into releasing the vehicle. Meatboy and the rest of the band waited six blocks away in a coffee shop for Paula to pick them up. None of them were particularly interested in being questioned in connection with the party on Commercial Drive, which was now being referred to as a riot. A couple of windows had been broken and several cars damaged, but you couldn't have a party that large without some kind of breakage.

Meatboy put his foot to the gas and zipped past an old lady crawling along in the passing lane. It was good to be back. His wound was healing nicely, and for a bonus he would have a cool scar to show for it. Problem was, during his recuperation he hadn't been able to get much done and the band had to leave town tomorrow. Typically, and despite many warnings from their manager, they had left everything to the last minute and still had a lot to do.

"Stop at McDonald's!" requested Atlas from the back seat. Despite Paula's suspicion that he was feeding a tape worm, eating remained high on his list of priorities. Tommy and the Rat were crammed into the little space remaining in the back and weren't happy about stopping anywhere.

"Fuck Ronald!" voiced Tommy. The idea of Atlas dripping special sauce all over him made his stomach do backflips.

"I don't know about McDonalds, but we gotta stop for gas. Maybe we can kill two birds with one stone," Meatboy suggested diplomatically. They were cruising down the highway on their way back from the airport, having just dropped off their manager who was flying out early to attend to tour details. Earlier, they had put their gear on the tour bus which was leaving today to be in L.A. tomorrow.

The Parisienne was running dangerously low on fuel. The big four-barrel sucked like a vampire at a nudist colony. Spotting a Husky stop, Meatboy swerved abruptly into the parking lot and stood on the brakes.

"Goddamn it!" complained the Rat nearly eating the head rest. "This ain't the bloody Autobahn, why do you always have to drive like a maniac?"

"Cause it's fun!" answered Meatboy climbing out of the car. By the time he had begun filling up, Atlas was already in the restaurant ordering cheeseburgers. Paula paused outside to stretch her legs. A newspaper headline from an outdoor vending machine caught her eye. Dropping some change into the box, she pulled out a paper and studied it with a mixture of shock and disbelief.

"Holy shit! Meatboy! Check this out!" She brought the paper over to him and thrust it under his nose.

Meatboy put the gas nozzle on autolock and took the paper. The headline read: SENIOR AID ADMITS TO LAND SPECULATION SCHEME IN CASE OF MISSING MINISTER.

Underneath was a large photograph of the whacked-out suit who had kidnapped Paula. Starting with the wrecked BMW abandoned on Broadway, a three column article detailed the events that had led up to the disappearance of the missing politician. It was both scandal and mystery. Indeed, it was a media event of international attention.

Meatboy quickly scanned the article and looked up at Paula. "So that's who that asshole was!" he exclaimed. "Looks like he fucked with the wrong people! I'll betcha a boot full of worms he went missing because of that money!"

"Sheeit!" said Paula, "Those guys play for keeps! No wonder he wanted it back so badly." Originally Paula thought he had been overreacting, after all it was only money—which reminded her. "By the way, I found your stash."

"What stash?" asked Meatboy. What the hell was she talking about?

Paula looked him squarely in the eye to see if he was trying to bullshit her. All she saw was a bewildered expression. "Ya mean to tell me you don't remember hiding twenty thousand dollars in my closet?" Only Meatboy could pull off such a bone-headed move.

"Oh yeah!" said Meatboy pretending to remember. "I was saving that for later! You don't think I would give away all the money, do you?"

The Boeing 747 rolled down the tarmac and jumped ponderously into the air. The members of Fire in the Hole stretched their legs luxuriously, flying first class. Already they were acting as if it were an everyday occurrence.

"Excuse me, Miss," asked Tommy. "Can I get some more champagne, please." At least he was being polite. The stewardess rushed to refill his glass.

Atlas was trying to be patient about being fed but he could see a serving cart laden with food and drink just beyond a curtain in the front of the cabin. A tantalizing aroma drifted down the aisle and teased his nose. He knew death from starvation must be near if airline food smelled good. When were they going to eat?

Tommy got to his feet, weaving slightly from the champagne and the altitude. "I'll go see if I can find out what the holdup is," he told Atlas. Brushing past the curtain, he stepped into the first-class serving compartment and looked around the dim interior. Nobody home. The food sat steaming under its plastic covers. Kneeling beside the cart, he made a few minor adjustments. You could never tell when a mini-crescent wrench key chain would come in handy. As he straightened to admire his handiwork, the stewardess snuck up behind him.

"Excuse me, sir. This area is for staff only."

"Huh? Oh, sure! I was just wondering when we were going to get some grub."

"The meal will be served shortly. If you'd like to return to your seat, I'll be right with you." She held the curtain open and indicated for him to sit down. Tommy stumbled down the aisle and took his seat behind Atlas and Meatboy. Anxiously, he awaited the arrival of the food cart. Finally the stewardess slid back the curtain and began serving dinner. Moving from front to back, the cart made its way slowly down the aisle. Tommy held his breath as he watched the left front wheel begin to wobble. Now the stewardess was only several seats away. Unnoticed by everyone except Tommy, the wheel came away from the cart and rolled underneath a seat. Miraculously the cart continued to function as before without tipping. C'mon...c'mon...he urged mentally, do it! The cart rolled on.

Shit, thought Tommy, It's not going to...

As the stewardess removed a soft drink, the balance shifted and the cart dumped trays of steaming food onto Meatboy and Atlas' startled laps. Keerashh! Lobster Newburg clung to the front of Meatboy's t-shirt like a plateful of squashed bugs. Atlas absently picked a chunk of lobster from his shirt and popped it in his mouth.

"Ha! Ha! Ha!" howled Tommy. Meatboy and Atlas were looking at him as though he was utterly and irredeemably mad. He flipped out of his seat and doubled over laughing hysterically in the aisle. Payback was sweet.

Below, the glittering lights of l.a. stretched beyond infinity.